COME BACK TO SORRENTO

COME BACK
TO SORRENTO

Originally published as

THE TENTH MOON

DAWN POWELL

INTRODUCTION BY TIM PAGE

STEERFORTH PRESS

SOUTH ROYALTON, VERMONT

Library of Congress Cataloging-in-Publication Data
Powell, Dawn.
[Tenth Moon]
Come back to Sorrento : The tenth moon / Dawn Powell;
introduction by Tim Page.
p.   cm.
Originally published: The tenth moon.
New York : Farrar & Rinehart, 1932.
ISBN 1–883642–26–4 (alk. paper)
1. Women music teachers — Ohio — Fiction.
2. Women singers — Ohio — Fiction.
3. Married Women — Ohio — Fiction.
4. Friendship — Ohio — Fiction.   I. Title
PS3531.0936T46   1997
813'.52 — dc21   97–29556 CIP

Manufactured in the United States of America
First Printing

DAWN POWELL was born in Mount Gilead, Ohio, the second daughter of Roy King Powell and Hattie Sherman Powell, on November 28, 1896. She ran away from home at the age of twelve and was raised by her aunt, Orpha May Sherman Steinbrueck, in Shelby, Ohio. She graduated from Lake Erie College with the class of 1918 and moved immediately to New York, where she lived and worked for the rest of her life. She was married to the advertising executive, Joseph R. Gousha, and they had one son, Joseph R. Gousha, Jr.

Powell published fifteen novels—*Whither* (1925), *She Walks In Beauty* (1928), *The Bride's House* (1929), *Dance Night* (1930), *The Tenth Moon* (1932), *The Story Of A Country Boy* (1934), *Turn, Magic Wheel* (1936), *The Happy Island* (1938), *Angels On Toast* (1940), *A Time To Be Born* (1942), *My Home Is Far Away* (1944), *The Locusts Have No King* (1948), *The Wicked Pavilion* (1954), *A Cage For Lovers* (1957), and *The Golden Spur* (1962). Her play "Jig-Saw" was published in 1936 and some of her numerous short stories were collected in *Sunday, Monday and Always* (1952).

At the time of Powell's death in 1965, virtually all of her books were out of print. With this publication of *Come Back to Sorrento (The Tenth Moon)* nine of Powell's novels are back in print, along with her widely acclaimed *The Diaries of Dawn Powell: 1931-1965*.

Introduction

Come Back To Sorrento is Dawn Powell's gentlest novel—a wise, sweet and sorrowful miniature that stands alone within the body of her work. It is yet another of her Ohio novels, but the action is set in a very different Ohio than we have come to know from her earlier books. In those works, Powell gave us the gritty, industrial life of the small city; now she immerses us in the honeysuckle, wild flowers, and autumn bonfires of the small town.

Powell began work on *Come Back To Sorrento* in early 1931, when she was living at 106 Perry Street in the far western edge of Greenwich Village. It was a difficult time for her; *Dance Night* had been released the previous autumn and, although it had received some admiring reviews and probably sold more copies than any of her earlier works, she was still deeply disappointed with its relative neglect. "It seems to me that ever since I finished *Dance Night* I have been marking time, waiting for something that doesn't happen," she wrote in her diary on July 20, 1931. "I can't buckle down seriously to a big job but just do little odd pieces—marking time, really, in my mind, waiting for *Dance Night* to come out with great éclat. As if it had never come out—a rocket that only sizzled because it was rained on.

Still wait for the blaze in the sky. It did a very funny thing to me, that dead rocket."

Although she hadn't yet realized it, Powell was already involved in three "big jobs" when she wrote these lines; she had started a preliminary version of *Turn, Magic Wheel* (which she would soon put aside until the middle of 1934), she was hard at work on *Come Back To Sorrento* (which she called "Madame Benjamin" in its planning stages), and she had just begun the magnificent diary that she would keep until the end of her life. In fact, the very first entry in that diary—on January 1, 1931— is a succinct early expression of the central theme of *Come Back To Sorrento:* "The tragedy of people who once were glamorous, now trying in mediocre stations to modestly refer to their pasts. Kind, stupid friends pity their 'lies' until grand relic must shout and brag, 'You see me in this little town—ah, but Bernhardt told me I was a great actress!' They brag only because no one believes anyone is more than he seems at the moment."

In time, Powell's heroine, whom she named Connie Benjamin, became a soprano, not an actress, and the compliment that sustained her came from a mythical singer known as the "great Morini," not Sarah Bernhardt. But the essence of the book is already there in embryo: *Come Back To Sorrento* is the study of thwarted artists and cosmopolites living in a small town that does not—cannot—understand aesthetics and ambition.

Connie's closest companion is the town's new music instructor, Blaine Decker, who has studied in Europe and therefore come to Dell River with a ready-made legend. The author and the contemporary reader (although not Connie or the townspeople) understand that Blaine is homosexual; without judgment or malice, Powell repeatedly uses what were even then coded expressions such as "queer," "gay," and "strange" in connection with him, while other characters speak of his dandy "mannerisms." Blaine, too, lives in the past, in the glowing recollection of an idyllic year in Paris, where his roommate was the successful novelist, Starr Donnell.

The two small-town sophisticates, misunderstood and sometimes mistrusted by their neighbors, create their own exclusive clique, a fantasy world built largely on imagined lives for themselves, past and future, beyond the borders of Dell River. They discuss music and literature, pass privileged judgment on visiting artists, and generally behave with a defensive pride that sometimes crosses into intellectual snobbery. Still, the author handles both characters with understanding and empathy throughout; anybody who has ever doubted the extent of Dawn Powell's compassion for human suffering should behold what she makes of Connie Benjamin and Blaine Decker.

Powell's wit is less pointed than in most of her works, although the acuity of her insight is never in doubt. On Connie's husband, the taciturn German carpenter Gus, for example: "She was fond of him because he seemed somehow the very kind husband of a dear friend, not her own husband at all." Or Mrs. Busch, who takes in washing for Dell River families: "Her casual references to her work made it seem that her long days of laundering were only a gentlewoman's hobby."

Come Back To Sorrento is a book without sharp edges. There are no real villains and Connie and Blaine are decidedly fragile heroes; neither has "the god-like ruthlessness so necessary to the genuine artist." The book is poignant, not tragic, and a tender fatalism pervades the action. "I've gone over the whole thing dozens of times and I always come to the same goal," Connie tells Blaine at their first meeting when he asks about her aborted career. "There never is any real choice about your life . . . just the one door open to you always . . . You can't say you're sorry."

Both Connie and Blaine hide their deepest fears and hauntings from each other. One of the odder quirks of Powell's diary is the way she dismisses the deaths of her father, her sister, and the aunt who raised her in clipped, simple, declarative sentences without any emotional elaboration. There is a passage in

Come Back To Sorrento that might serve as her explanation: "You cannot talk about real things, there are no words for genuine despair, there are not even tears, there is only a heavenly numbness for which to pray and upon that gray curtain words may dance as words were intended to do, fans and pretty masks put up to shield the heart."

Throughout the creation of *Come Back To Sorrento*, Powell seems to have had mixed feelings about its worth. "This new novel seems to ring true but it is not anything important or unusual," she wrote in June, 1931. "It runs along easily and solely by intuition, unlike the careful, solid planning of *Dance Night*. It is very slight—as thin and usual as the works of Ellen Glasgow or Isa Glenn—so easy I scarcely miss what goes out of my brain. I neither like nor dislike it. I only feel that if I were stronger and not so crippled by the disappointment of *Dance Night*, my domestic panic and responsibilities, I could do bigger stuff than this light lady-writing."

By the time the novel was ready for publication Powell had decided that it simply wasn't very good. Her growing dislike was compounded when Farrar & Rinehart, her publishers, rejected her title—"Come Back To Sorrento"—and issued the book in the fall of 1932 as *The Tenth Moon*, a phrase taken from the line from Shelley that serve as the book's epigram. "How I wish they would have allowed me to call it 'Come Back To Sorrento,' " Powell complained. "Since one gets so little else for one's work, a title that pleases the writer seems such a little boon to ask . . . *The Tenth Moon* —how I hate the empty, silly, pointless title!—is an excellent, lucidly written book—above the average, point for point, the only thing I've ever done completely on brain power—a correct book—a work that can be measured with all the proper rulers—therefore no margin of wonder in it, therefore not a vital living work."

A year later, unhappy over the paucity of serious critical attention paid to her work, she briefly determined to give up any high literary ambitions and write only "to find a public somewhere for something, if it's only in *Snappy Stories* or *The New Yorker*. Write *Tenth Moon* crap if that's as much reality as people can stand."

The *Tenth Moon* sold less than 3,000 copies and there were only a few reviews, most of them short and poorly placed, albeit generally positive in tone. The most perceptive notice was by a distinguished critic and editor, Harold E. Stearns, published in the *New York Herald Tribune*. "It is neither the characters, nor their fates, pathetic or gay, which linger in one's memory after closing the book," Stearns wrote, "but rather the peculiar penumbrae of feeling in which they are enwrapped, like melodies not quite remembered nor yet wholly lost. Compared with the clatter of events, the almost aggressively picaresque flow of episode, in most current fiction, The *Tenth Moon* comes as a particularly compelling, a particularly gracious interlude." Stearns called special attention to "as simple and poignant a death scene as I have read for a long time"; I, too, find this one of the author's very finest set pieces—a faltering, evanescent vision of death from the dying character's point of view.

For years, Powell thought this one of her poorest books. Then, in 1943, finding herself stymied in the middle of writing *My Home Is Far Away*, she went back and reread her copy of *The Tenth Moon*, hoping that it might provide some direction. She was shocked by what she found: "I was actually absorbed in it and read it all the way through weeping and moved to my depths. The fact is that it is a beautiful book—the best writing I ever did and technically flawless, with the most delicate flowering of a relationship that grips interest far more than my dramatic plots such as [*Story of a*] *Country Boy*. I then examined my notes in my journal and found all the way through references to the pleasure of writing something that left my emotions absolutely uninvolved, a mere craftsmanship job, a literary joke—okay, critics, I won't give you a pound of flesh, I will cheat you. Result: a quivering book filled with pain and beauty."

Almost 70 years after it was begun, it is a pleasure to present that "quivering book" for the first time under Powell's own title—*Come Back To Sorrento*.

Tim Page
Lakewood, Ohio
June 4, 1997

EVENINGS she sat on the porch hidden from the street by honeysuckle and morning-glory vines, through their tangled foliage she watched the sun go down and gray light change to a black screen on which the vine-leaves gleamed in a silvery frosted pattern. She swung slowly back and forth in the hammock, one foot under her, the other rhythmically touching the porch floor, it was swing, tap, swing, tap; one movement released her fancy, sent her soaring through years but the tapping of her slipper brought her back. You are here! here! here! it reminded her.

The house grew dark and quiet, drew the lilac bushes into its shadow, made room in its silence for the creaking of the hammock and the tap of the woman's slipper on the porch floor. Tonight the smell of burning leaves carried insistently over the fragrance of dead lilacs and drying shrubs. Down the street she caught glimpses of bonfires, the firelight illumining the faces of watching children. She saw the parade of bonfires growing smaller and smaller in the distance, mere blots of gold in the blackness, spangling the honeysuckle vine with their reflections.

The creaking of the hammock came to a gentle stop and with the pause the high shrill murmur of children's voices, blended by distance into one long sustained soprano note, crept closer. The eager prolonged note was like a bell, for Connie Benjamin it was a call to Now, to Here, to what was really true. She went to the porch steps and sat down on the stoop. The moss-rosebush she had planted when she first moved here had grown up the porch trellis beside the steps, its tiny thorns daintily scratched her arm as she adjusted her skirts. One petrified bud remained on its stem but its moment had come for when Connie touched it the very heart fell softly apart, its petals scattered in a little ghostly flutter over the dying bush and over the folds of her dress. She brushed them off and the thorns caught her hand again. She was glad of the sharp tingling pain, it was the tingle of life at least and she had been so far away. Sometimes she wondered if there could be a limit to these twilight voyages, if some day she would stray too far and there would be no bridge nor bell to bring her home.

Bonfires wavered, embers glowed here and there and went out, streetlamps measured the darkness far up the hill and were stopped by the waiting woods, lights blocked out amber windows against the night. Groups of children fluttered past the house in a flurry of breathless laughter, their blurred light figures separated and vanished into different gateways. Connie heard Helen's voice above the others and Mimi's lower-pitched response. It reminded her again that the masks of evening cannot hold for long, no matter how blind one wishes to be. . . . She went indoors and turned on the living-room table-light, then into the parlor and switched on the piano-lamp. The array of music with her own old study book on the rack pleased her as it always did. The page was turned to Lesson XV—"The Chapel in the Forest." Standing up, one foot on the soft pedal, she tried a few treble bars. The piano jangled gaily, and obligingly carried on a little echoing tune of its own between Connie's fumbling chords. Even Mimi could play better than that for all her square, practical little hands. That was the trouble, either your imagination stopped with the practical limits of your own accomplishment as Mimi's did, or you gave up even trying because you heard the real music, you had inside yourself the feeling for a chapel in the forest, the pure solemn charm of a prayer in primeval wilderness; why destroy a perfect image with the distortions of one's erring fingers?

On the porch she heard the girls talking to someone. Suddenly the thought of her two children made Connie's throat swell, she ached with love for them, love that was like a farewell to some joy gone or soon to be gone forever rather than pride of possession; they seemed almost but not quite hers, hers to touch but not to hold. For that matter nothing in the world ever seemed irrevocably or tangibly hers. This room. . . . she had selected the curtains, the oak reading table, the brown rigidly stuffed sofa, even the classic mezzotints on the wall, the flowered brown carpet, the ferns, the hanging baskets in the window, but it was not hers. She took a detached pleasure in its old known comfort, as if she were a visitor doing her best to adapt herself to a strange and not displeasing environment. . . . Gus was not hers, nor any part of her. She was fond of him because he seemed somehow the very kind husband of a dear friend, not her own husband at all. What belonged to her and was hers was the period from supper till dark when she played with her life, shaped it this way and that. The figures of this hand-wrought dream world were drawn from memory and fancy, they fell into whatever roles she appointed like familiar toy soldiers. This was the life she controlled, over which she constantly triumphed. She expected nothing from the other because there she was only a polite spectator and naturally the prizes were reserved for the participants.

She drew the piano bench under her and sat down. As her fingers moved softly over the keys improvising chords and runs she began to hum an air. The humming swelled fuller and then lost itself in a rumbling of bass chords. The piano tinkled resolutely, the keyboard wobbled stiffly from right to left like a concert singer getting the utmost from her diaphragm. Connie

closed her lips and the humming went on vibrantly, it seemed
not to come from her throat but from one string, her whole
body was the instrument. The light soft song soared through
the rooms, echoes of it strung out like lanterns through the hall
and shadowy corners. It was not a song at all but a gentle lovely
purring sound that held to no pattern, and from the street
seemed not a human voice but echoes coming from the walls of
a haunted house. When Mimi was a baby it had made her cry,
this purr, and even at twelve it caught at Mimi's heart, made her
lag behind Helen in the shadow of the porch vine, somehow
sorry for her mother and wanting to give her some consoling
gift, something so wonderful she could not even picture it,
something improbable like the last dying bonfire, or the Sunday
sun coming through church windows.

Helen turned at the doorway to give Mimi a significant
look, a nod toward the street, and Mimi heard the last of the
children passing the house on their way home. As they ran they
hummed shrilly and derisively, mocking Connie Benjamin's
melody with discords.

ℐ

Everyone knew Mrs. Benjamin. They knew she was not snobbish — she was far too gentle for that and in actual material
possessions had less than her neighbors; her aloofness was not
due to a sense of superiority but very likely to shyness. No one
could blame a woman for natural reserve though often people
speculated on how any human being could live fifteen years in
one village without friends or confidantes. Helen, in school,
heard these comments and reproached her mother more and
more for the cardinal sin of being different.

"I must try and talk to people," Connie would tell herself.
"For the girls' sake I must live more outside the family."

It was bad enough, said Helen, for one's father never to say
more than five words to anyone, but one's mother ought to mix

with the other girls' mothers and know how the Commencement dresses were being made this year, what was being served
at birthday parties... a mother, really, Helen said, ought to be a
help to a girl. Mimi, who was only twelve, said nothing to all
this, her loyalty to her mother lost in her fear of her sister.

Connie had had spurts of friendliness periodically but since
they sprang from no interest whatever in people but from the
prickings of conscience, her shy ventures came to little. She was
relieved in a way, for the failure of her slight efforts allowed her
to bask in her own society without compunction. She sometimes conversed with Mrs. Busch with the vague feeling that
Mrs. Busch was Dell River and once established with her she
was established with the town.

Mrs. Busch lived up the alley beside the Benjamins' house.
She was a large, silent blonde woman with pale, white-lashed
blue eyes; a wart blighted her nose. She was not really a washerwoman. She just "did a few little things up for Mrs. Tracy" or
someone else; her casual references to her work made it seem
that her long days of laundering were only a gentlewoman's
hobby. Busch drove the Central Delivery and looked exactly like
his wife. When he brought groceries to a kitchen where his wife
happened to be washing, Mrs. Busch would go outside the back
door with him and they would confer in low, grave voices over
some great crisis in Central Delivery or a deep problem in laundry.

When Connie would go downtown or on a walk through
the country she took the alley shortcut and stopped at Mrs.
Busch's gate. A lovely day. . . . Yes, it was, Mrs. Busch would
grant, her mouth full of clothespins, her fat red hands hanging
up a wet sheet. . . . And warm for September. . . . Indeed, indeed,
admitted Mrs. Busch without looking up. . . . The garden looks
charming. . . . Why not, after all the work the mister put into it,
Mrs. Busch would politely retort, he don't leave it alone a
minute. . . . There is a song about a garden, Connie would say—
she wished she could remember the words, but it's so long since
she studied. At this point Mrs. Busch would invariably state

that her daughter, Honey, sang very well. It was amazing since she and the mister neither one could carry a tune. Connie showed interest—neither of her own girls could sing. Wasn't it a pity when she herself had studied voice abroad and had sung once for Morini himself? Yes sir, she might have sung in grand opera, Mrs. Busch, but it was not to be. . . .

"Is that so?" Mrs. Busch always politely asked, but not surprised since after all she'd heard this announcement practically every time Mrs. Benjamin stopped by.

One morning Mrs. Busch added to their well-known conversational routine by introducing further proof of Honey's vocal talent. The new school music-teacher had said she sang well. He had studied abroad, too, just as Mrs. Benjamin claimed to have done.

Connie felt a rush of excitement at this news. Another artist like herself. Where was he living? What was his name?

"His name's Decker," answered Mrs. Busch, "and he didn't take the house on Mulberry Street that the school music-teacher nearly always takes. He claimed it was too big. So he took those rooms over Mr. Benjamin's shop. Must not have any family."

Mrs. Busch made no further comment on the professor's choice of residence, but Connie knew the cheap little rooms over the cobbler shop were not what the village expected of its music teachers. Even if the man lived alone, even though the rooms were pleasant enough and near the school, they were not suitable, he should have rented a house. Such patent economy looked queer.

"Yes sir, he says, 'that little girl of yours, Mrs. Busch, is quite a singer,' that's what he told me," said Mrs. Busch, adjusting the clothes pole so that the great white sheets rose high in the air like a stage backdrop ascending the wings, leaving Mrs. Busch the enormous, ugly performer against the standard overpainted house curtain of green lilac and elderberry bushes, gray woodsheds and chicken houses, and brilliant blue sky peeping through a froth of white clouds.

Connie hesitated at the gate, anxious to say something very kind and friendly to show that she did not think Mrs. Busch was almost frightening in her ugliness. She wanted to compliment her on Honey, too, without shivering as she did when she thought of the poor child.

"I'm sure she must have talent," she finally plunged.

Mrs. Busch showed no gratitude over her neighbor's comment, she was perfectly complacent over Honey and needed reassurance from no one. Connie never got over her first glimpse of Honey—a golden-haired, incredibly exquisite child then, the loveliest child she had ever seen, dancing around a group of the other children, thumbing her nose at them, and finally whirling herself dizzily round and round down the street, screaming with laughter. Crazy Honey. . . . Yes, she did have a voice as the new music teacher had said—a high, hollow choir-boy voice that soared and glided like nothing on earth, and hearing that sometimes echoing through the alley, Connie shivered and did not know why.

"I shouldn't be surprised if Honey ended up on the stage," said Mrs. Busch, picking up her empty clothes-basket and starting for her kitchen porch. "The mister says he wouldn't bat an eye if she turned out to be a kinda Marylinn Miller or something. It isn't as if she couldn't dance, too."

Mrs. Busch's calm ignoring of her daughter's strangeness was almost as frightening as the antics of the seraphic-faced girl.

"Well, I must go on downtown," Connie said. "Mr. Benjamin expects me."

She felt, as always, slightly dashed that Mrs. Busch merely nodded a polite acceptance of her good-bye, never urging her to pause for further conversation or betraying any interest in her destination. For Connie these interchanges were practices in friendship and sociability, but each encounter with Mrs. Busch made her conscious of her own failure, something in herself must block the way, for certainly she'd seen this curious woman chattering most eagerly with other inhabitants of the village.

Her face reddened slightly as she hurried up the cinder-strewn alley to the main street, she restored her poise by the thought of how ridiculous it was to attempt breaking the social reserve of the town washerwoman, as if in Mrs. Busch was concentrated the very heart of Dell River society. Whatever she represented her polite reticence sent Connie flying back into her own shell, unwilling to emerge for contacts with others. She hurried down the main street, smiling back at women who called greetings to her from their doorways or front yards, but not risking further defeat by bowing to them first.

Summer was over once again and all along the street boys were raking up leaves for the evening bonfires; little houses warmed themselves in the scarlet glory of overhanging maples, hydrangeas gloomily cherished their last rusty blossoms, and withering hedges shrunk back from the little white fences they had concealed all summer long. Even after fifteen years Connie was often on the point of exclaiming, "What a nice village you have here, you other people"—for she did love its quiet streets, its peace, but again as the tourist might. She did not know the names of the streets or more than a dozen of its citizens, for she had vaguely felt that in her brief stay here such knowledge was unnecessary. She always paused at the town square, puzzled until she could decide which turn brought her to Gus' shop.

Crossing the little park she met Mr. Busch, himself, and a few people hurrying home from their morning's shopping with bulging paper market-bags. Some bowed to her and some only stared, but Connie felt them all turning to look after her. She was no longer troubled by this interest. A long time ago she had thought it was because she was a stranger from an eastern city or perhaps because she had almost been an opera star. Now she realized it was only because she wore hat and gloves every time she left her house, whereas other women ran downtown in aprons, bareheaded unless it was a club day or a school or church occasion.

The town buildings in Dell River were old, few changes
had been made for decades beyond the new wing on the school-
house, for manual training and domestic sciences inaugurated a
few years back. Occasionally a modern pink-stuccoed cottage
popped out among the older shingled residences but not many,
for the town's population had not grown since it was founded.
A small foundry, a few garages, a candy factory, a sawmill and
flour mill, these were practically the town's only industries
unless you counted the enormous nurseries just outside the city
limits, whose trading in irises was the only cogent reason for
trains to stop here. As a matter of fact the newest building was
the little two-story brick building bearing the sign:

AUGUST BENJAMIN
NEW SHOES FOR SALE
OLD SHOES REPAIRED

Benjamin had built the place twelve years ago, but women
sending their children to the cobbler's still directed them to the
little "new" building around the corner. It was squeezed
between the candy sales building and the Gas Company as if it
had no more business being there than a weed pushing up
through the cracks of a city sidewalk. The two large rooms
downstairs were Mr. Benjamin's place of business, while the
three rooms upstairs, accessible by a separate door at the left of
the main entrance, had been rented as living and business quarters to a dentist for several years. That busy little man had
finally transferred himself to Pittsburgh and until today Connie
had not learned of the successor to his quarters.

She glanced in the show window at the ancient display of
rubber soles, shoe polish, galoshes and the "new footwear" con-
sisting of four pairs of ladies' stout, high-topped black shoes
purchased eight years ago at a warehouse fire sale and ever since
on display as a concession to his daughter's ambition for something a little better than a plain cobbler father. Connie herself

obligingly took on a pair of the new shoes every winter but there were no other customers for the Sales Department.

She saw Gus in the back of the shop bending over his work-table. In the dark of the shop and contrasting with his dark brown apron his reddish hair and close-cropped burnished beard seemed radiantly out of place, and from the gleam of his sea-blue eyes Connie thought he might be creating some mighty epic instead of a pair of French heels. In his Sunday clothes, neatly pressed, she often thought he looked less a cobbler than a university professor or a foreign diplomat. August, whether or no he resembled these distinguished figures, considered his own trade quite as dignified as theirs and if he had borne a son would have wished no better fate than a cobbler's for him, so that the line of Benjamins in that trade should not be broken. Seven generations of Benjamin cobblers was a matter of more pride than one university diploma or a single portfolio of public office.

"That is quite true," Connie had thought long ago, a bride eager to be proud of her husband for whatever reasons he wished, and she had sustained this belief in the worthiness of craftsmanship, trying to impress it upon her daughters, who, as they grew up, resented delivering boots to their school-chums, or being asked to mind the store while Papa went home to lunch. If he had only owned the Candy Kitchen, as Mr. Herbert did, endowing his daughters thus with deathless popularity, or the Dry Goods Store, or better yet, the Music Store. . . . What social advantage in school came to little girls whose only fortune was their excellent half-soles?

"The new music professor wants the upstairs fitted out a little more," Benjamin told his wife when she came back to him. "Curtains—cushions—a few things like that. You can see when you go up. He says he has some furnishings of his own, too, but not quite enough. Go up and see what he needs as soon as he comes in."

Connie sat down gingerly on a wooden bench. The smell of leather and polish made her a little dizzy but she had never told

Gus. He paid no more attention to her but hammered away at the slipper heels, his red brows meeting in a frown of concentration. Connie looked out the one back-window at the little brick-paved court behind the shop. One fallen leaf was caught in a cobweb spread across the window, through this delicate, silver-threaded wheel she saw the gnarled, rheumatic branches of the old apple tree, no longer making any pretense of pushing toward heaven but curling its roots in comfortable resignation to age and fate. Its mighty gesture had been made, after all, years ago when it pushed its roots up through the brick paving. Now the gray blighted roots were humped into a semblance of gray toes bursting out of their worn old boots, a fitting monument to Benjamin's establishment. Wooden stairs went from this back court to the apartment upstairs, though the regular entrance was through the tiny vestibule in front.

Keeping her eyes fixed on the cobweb, Connie did not mind the musty odor of the shop. She did not talk to Gus, partly because he believed in silence and partly because there was so little they had to say to each other that they must spend their words very cautiously if they were to last them a life-time. Sometimes Connie had a rush of reminiscences, confidences, and hopes—she would talk feverishly for hours to Gus' quiet "That's right. . . . Sure . . . oh, sure . . . you bet . . . uh-huh . . . yeah . . . sure . . . that so . . . well, well." Worn out finally by beating against this calm wall Connie would fall asleep, consoling herself with the thought that however inarticulate he was Gus understood, his silence was not a cold barrier but fundamental understanding. . . . She remembered the music teacher.

"What's his name, Gus?" she asked.

Gus wrinkled his brows and then answered, "Decker's the name. Blaine Decker. Professor Blaine Decker."

She was thinking of the blue curtains she could put in his living room when the music teacher appeared in the shop. He was a slight, brusque little man with a tiny moustache which he twisted constantly; his gray suit needed pressing badly and this, with his longish thin fair hair gave him a surprisingly unkempt appearance. But his eyes and manner were so perfectly confident, his voice so assured, almost commanding, that one ended by being vaguely impressed that here was a somebody, there was no mistaking that. Let him be shabby, let him live over the humblest cobbler shop, this man was sufficiently a personage to do as he jolly well pleased, so Connie thought.

He bowed to her in a curiously foreign manner, clicking his heels, then devoted himself to a discussion with Gus of keys, ventilation, hot water heating, and all the time his brilliant blue eyes strayed absently toward Mrs. Benjamin, until unconsciously her head drooped and her face grew scarlet. A few minutes later she was guiding him through the upstairs apartment, discussing blue curtains and bed linen.

"I won't need much," he explained carefully. "You see I have all my own things—bits of tapestry, all the little things you pick up abroad. I studied in Leipzig and Paris, you see . . . I intended to be a concert pianist . . . However. . . ."

At his words Connie's heart swelled with unknown excitement, for a moment she had the curious sensation of having invented this character for her evening fancies, it was almost too difficult to bring him from her ideal into her actual world. Now it was like meeting another exile in a strange land, a fellow countryman, and all the treasured experiences locked away from the blank gaze of the world could be freed for these familiar understanding eyes. Phrases of the old language came stiffly to mind, so stiffly that all she could do was to stand in the sunporch (to be curtained in yellow, he decided) and smile at him.

"Your husband is German, isn't he?" he inquired. "And you—you belong to Dell River?"

"Indeed no—I'm a stranger here, too, Mr. Decker. You see I am—or was—a musician, also," Connie confessed in a rush. "I studied in convents in the East, then I sang one day before Morini, who was to teach me. I might have gone into grand opera, perhaps."

"No! Is it possible!" The professor's violent amazement was not at all like Dell River's skeptical acceptance of the same words and Connie's heart pounded in gratitude.

"Girls are foolish. For instance I—I ran away instead. I was confused, only seventeen, and such a great man to compliment me. . . . I was trapped by my own excitement, don't you see . . . I ran away . . . married . . . and . . ."

"You ran away with Benjamin, eh?" He did not wait for an answer, assuming that of course this was the case so Connie did not set him right. It was too complicated for explanation, the story of herself and Tony. Easier to let people believe there had never been anyone but Gus. . . .

"That's the way with women as artists," he said, "always throwing their careers on the rubbish pile for some man. . . . So now, here you are. . . . Never hear an opera—or concert—"

Connie was made bold in her excitement.

"How about you? What about your career, too? You talk about women, but after all what are you doing teaching music in a public school?"

"A different story." He turned abruptly away and then, as Connie flushed, feeling rebuffed, he smiled at her. "I'll tell it to you, some time, don't worry."

He opened a packing case and took out some china carefully wrapped in rags, a battered copper samovar, a cracked terra cotta dancing figure, a moth-eaten Paisley shawl. He proudly held out a small satinwood box for her to examine, and twisted the key in its lock.

"There's nothing like having one's own things, is there? Look." He pulled some bits of yellowed lace from the interior of the box and waited for her cry of admiration, but Connie was obliged to beg his forgiveness for not knowing lace—lace or glass. His face fell. That was the way with women, he complained, they never appreciated their own subjects. It was outrageous, all the things they might and should be but *would* not. Even his mother—here he pulled out a silver-framed

photograph and placed it on the little oak desk beside the sunporch doorway—yes, even she neglected the charming
opportunities of a woman's life to raise dogs. Dogs, according to
his mother, probably the most unreasonable person in the
world, were more fascinating than old china, and an automobile road map was more beautiful than an opera score. . . . All
the time he was adjusting the pictured profile of the handsome
woman so that it would show to advantage. He wiped off the
glass with his sleeve.

"Why did you come here?" Connie found herself asking
him. "There must be better places than this near New York—if
you must teach school."

He bent over the packing-case and drew out a blue cream-
pitcher with a broken handle and set it with infinite care on
the table.

"Wedgewood. . . . I did have the tea-pot once but a maid
broke it. . . . Why, bigger schools want better teachers, Mrs.
Benjamin. After all I'm not trained in the teaching end. I
bluffed a few years in a Southern high school, that's all—good
enough experience for here but not for city schools. It's not bad,
after all, because I gave up the great concert hero idea long ago.
When one has a mother to support—"

"It was a baby that stopped me from going on," Connie said.

"You poor child! Then stuck forever out here in the
woods, eh?" The pity welling in his bright compassionate eyes
was so much that it frightened Connie. She had never wanted
pity, she only wished to explain. Pity? Surely she was too fortunate a woman to warrant that, she was not lost, and pity was
for lost souls. She was so unprepared for the understanding
in his eyes that her own eyes blurred unexpectedly and there
was an ominous tingling in her head as if old thoughts long
stored in the attic were being creakily dragged out for this
season's use.

"It's a lovely town—you'll like it," she said, striving for
safer ground. "After all I've been very happy here, Professor

Decker, for nearly sixteen years. People are kind. And I have my children."

"I know. Good-bye to everything but house and food and family—that's what you mean." Connie flushed, bewildered at his sharpness. He went on, without noticing her. "Can I get a piano up here? The school promised me one—I saw the music store on the Square, didn't I?"

He was unpacking great piles of music, torn manuscripts, worn study books. Connie got to her knees and picked them up as they slid from his arms, merely handling them gave her indescribable happiness. She studied a page here and there eagerly; though what she had once known was long forgotten, she pronounced the composer's name to herself, as if the burning love for all music would magically endow her with knowledge, as if before the jumble of black notes and strange names a light would miraculously flare up in her mind, gates would swing wide, all would be known and long familiar to her. Sitting on the floor, arranging the scattered pages she began to hum softly, then stopped suddenly to look up at him.

"When I finished singing that day for him he said, 'Bravo! A glorious voice, Manuel,'" she said. "Manuel was my teacher. He had known Morini before, you see. I was only seventeen and I'd never really applied myself. But after that I knew I must. All the way going back to my grandfather's—Manuel and I talked of nothing but my future. I couldn't sleep for days. It was ghastly coming down from being treated like a great star to being treated like a child by my grandfather. . . . So, a week later I eloped and—"

It seemed so natural to be telling all this to him, for they knew each other, they seemed to have always known each other. Connie got to her feet and put the music on the study table. The stranger lit a cigarette thoughtfully and leaned back against the arm of the one easy chair.

"And you're sorry?"

Connie shook her head.

"No—I don't see how I could ever have done any differently. You know the way a person's made . . . I've gone over the whole thing dozens of times and I always come to the same goal . . . there never is any real choice about your life . . . just the one door open to you always. . . . You can't say you're sorry."

"Well, of course Benjamin is all right," he agreed, then feeling that this was almost rude in his understatement he hastened to add, "You can see he's unusually decent—the quiet protector type, the refuge after a terrific disappointment."

"That was it." Connie nodded and hesitated over the implied lie, but somehow she couldn't tell him that it had been Tony, not Gus Benjamin that she'd run away with. She couldn't—after telling him of her high youthful ambition—tell him about the street carnival in the little New England town and Tony in silver tights, how they'd run softly over the great moonlit lawn, remembering to keep his dark coat over her white dress, pausing in the pointed shadows of the little balsam trees to catch their breath and look back toward her grandfather's window, then stumbling on to the main road, waiting in the glare of automobile headlights for the bus to pick them up, clutching each other's trembling fingers. . . . No, Connie couldn't explain to Decker about Tony. After eighteen years she couldn't explain it even to herself . . . there are no alternatives in life, that was all she could say, one does the thing there is to do. . . .

Going downstairs back to the shop her lips moved unconsciously continuing an imaginary conversation with Decker, telling him all about Grandfather, about Manuel and the convent, changing the truth into suitable words, pouring her thirty-five years into sentences that would explain her life complete (except for Tony) so that they could begin afresh with this day. Her mind leaped to furnish Decker's own life up to this moment. She saw him in foreign cities—Munich, Leipzig, she saw him in stiff little German parks and then on sidewalk cafes in Paris, in casement-windowed salons playing the piano so beautifully she could weep for thinking of it. Little adventures unwound marvelously before her, composites of motion pictures she had seen, books she had read, and she even saw herself in these pictures, herself and Tony. Yes, Tony. She was surprised to find Tony here, willy-nilly, but why not, since though it was Decker's past, these were familiar scenes to her imagination, they were built years ago with Tony and there was no getting him out now.

༉

In bed the two girls whispered of school, of the music teacher, of the new boys. In their stiff cotton nightgowns, their thin young arms under their heads they lay, careful not to touch each other, only in sleep tumbling unconsciously into each other's arms. They went to bed at ten but whispered until twelve, remembering through all their confidences to tell each other nothing for they were sisters.

Helen, at fifteen, resented her parents, collected little grievances against them and spread them out at night like so many trophies and Mimi, being twelve, was torn between loyalty for her parents and dazed admiration for one who escaped such unconventional feelings. It was Mimi who stayed awake long after Helen had drawn her long legs up and fallen asleep. Mimi, wide awake, stared at the dim shadows the mirror helped the intruding starlight to create and wondered if Helen really would run away some day to Cincinnati or Chicago or New York as she threatened, if she really would ask Papa for twenty dollars for dancing lessons as her right, if she really would demand that Mama remain upstairs when some boy came to see her. Then would come the wave of love for Mama, stronger than any feeling for Helen or anything in the world. She was not jealous of Helen for being the pretty Benjamin girl, she did not think much about her own square homely little face, she did not mind so much walking home from school alone while Helen ran with a laughing admiring crowd. Mimi's romance concerned her mother and not herself at all.

She had made up a glamorous past for her mother, she swelled with pride over the little triumphs of Connie's past, made new ones to fill out the gaps. Beauty, to Mimi, meant her mother's face, clear, wide-apart brown eyes, sharply cut nose and oddly full lips, a rather thin pointed face softened by rich chestnut hair. There was to Mimi something fine, soft and perfumed about her mother, she was fascinated by the operatic gestures of long white hands, the throbbing excitement of her voice, the ever-present hint that some day the witches' spell would be broken and the Snow Queen herself, no longer disguised as Connie Benjamin, would emerge gloriously triumphant. Mimi saw her mother always on a swell of music, she saw her on a stage in a magic circle of light with swaying figures holding out their hands to her, she could hear her mother humming through it all, while radiant maidens floated over rainbows of heavenly music. She was ever dazzled that the enchanted one should be her mother, she could not understand how Helen could be so casual, often so cynical about this miracle.

"That old picture of her in the ermine jacket," Helen complained. "She wasn't much older than I am. Why don't I have fur coats then? Maybe if She'd had to wear an old sweater under a blue serge coat for two winters when she was a girl she'd understand more about me. And if she went away to boarding school, why shouldn't I?"

Mimi, not at all offended that this injustice did not extend to her but was only directed at Helen, whispered logical explanations.

"She should have thought of all that and about her children when she quarreled with her family," Helen retorted gloomily. "I get just furious thinking of all the things we might have had if she'd had more common sense. You too, Mimi—you could have had your hair permanent-waved like Estelle Mills and be quite pretty."

This was a stab in the dark but it went home, for Mimi's private theory was that curly hair would have made up for all other defects of feature. For Helen to guess this startled her and made it seem an absolute fact instead of mere theory. A brief resentment came over her for the mother whose magnificent gestures cost her daughter personal beauty, but Mimi dismissed it at once as a wicked idea. Even Helen relented a little on second thoughts. Today the new music teacher (freak though he was, all the girls said so) had singled her out from the whole class to be leader of the school chorus. She was to have charge of the class music every day except on the lesson day the way Rena Blake had done last year. Miss Murrell, the old dumb-bell, had said, "But Professor Decker, Helen isn't one of our strongest voices, you know," and he said right to her face and before the whole class, "That's all right, Miss Murrell, her mother is musically trained and I trust to background in these matters." Miss Murrell had plainly wanted Rena Blake for leader again. It was a come-down when old Decker spoke up that way.

"It was all because Mama was almost a great musician," Mimi told Helen breathlessly. "You've got to admit that, Helen. And maybe he knew her in those days."

"No, he didn't," Helen answered and then turned over toward the wall, punched her pillow into the right shape and prepared now for sleep. "How would he have known her then?"

Mimi lifted her head, leaned on her elbow.

"Why not when they were both abroad? Maybe he heard her singing for that great man—Morini?"

Helen yawned and pulled the covers up to her chin.

"Don't tell me you really believed that story," she said sleepily, and then added, while fear froze in Mimi's wondering heart. "Nobody else ever did . . . and certainly not me."

౨

The dinner for Professor Decker was a problem. Connie wanted a touch of formality about it but this was hard to achieve in Dell River where one was not invited a week ahead of time unless it was a holiday banquet. Usually dining with friends was impromptu and nothing more than taking pot-luck with neighbors before an evening at cards. Connie had taken no part in these casual entertainments so that Gus was surprised to find her so concerned over the proper way to entertain his tenant. Why should he be asked to dine, they never had mixed with the teachers before, what was the idea of it now? Connie ceased to discuss the occasion with him but planned it carefully in secret. She had never had any good table linen or china, so she decided to use the batiked piano scarf as a tablecloth and by having a Sunday night supper she could use her yellow china tea set. She had no new clothes for years but finally she dyed her old pink lace and satin negligee a deep gray, it looked quite like the tea gowns one saw in the magazines. She was never a good cook but Helen could fix things very nicely and had promised to make chicken à la king.

For days Connie worried about this great occasion. Mimi and Helen insisted on demanding the why and wherefore of it, they were mystified at Mama asking strangers in and Helen bitterly complained that their house was too shabby for those out-of-town teachers to visit. Old Decker would tell the Herberts and the principal (Helen liked Don Marshall, the principal's son) that the Benjamins had no glassware, just used old jelly glasses at the table, and he would make fun to everyone of their having overhead glaring lights instead of floor lamps and bridge lamps the way other people did. These shortcomings were all Connie's fault even more than they were a question of economy, for Connie was blind as a man to little household touches outside of color and light and general effect. It had never occurred to her, as it did so often to Helen, that there was much difference between her own home and other Dell River homes aside, of course, from Laurie Neville's great barren mansion out by the nurseries. That was what one should have, but between that Victorian museum and the simplest workman's cottage Connie saw no gradations, one had one or the other and she saw no way of softening the contrast, nor any reason to bemoan it before now. One was what one was and one had what one had. But now she saw everything with the stranger's eye and was vaguely dissatisfied. She was sorry she had made no friends in Dell River, for it made her gesture toward Decker seem too important to the family. She ended by inviting Helen's English teacher, Miss Murrell, since she had called twice about the girls' school work and had talked to Mrs. Benjamin confidentially about her own desire to write. She had even showed her the letters she had written home from France during the war when she had been a canteen worker. Connie, to whom writing was an almost impossible and not very important art, had been impressed by the other woman's ease in expressing thoughts and facts, and when she showered her with the sincerest praise the guest suddenly burst into tears. Connie stood helpless while the teacher, tears streaming down her face and hiccoughing little sobs, gathered her beloved letters together and fastened them in the gold-trimmed blue leather notebook again. At the door Miss Murrell had, after a final dab at her red eyes, squeezed Connie's hand and murmured, "I can't tell you how much this has meant to me—your saying that. No one ever—I mean—you know—here away from everything you might say—and—I thank you—oh I do thank you."

Then, bursting into tears again, she had run out of the house. That had been last spring. Connie hadn't seen her after that. The teachers usually went away in the summer, and somehow they had not met again. Connie had been more than a little frightened to see such a pale, quiet little person torn by such dreadful sobs, they were not like ordinary cries at all, not the gentle moans of a woman used to weeping, but hoarse, horrible noises like those of an animal in pain. By this time the memory of the awkward occasion was decently dimmed for both women, so Connie issued and Miss Murrell accepted the invitation without undue embarrassment.

"I wish," Connie said at breakfast, "that you girls would try to talk about classes as little as possible because that's what Mr. Decker wants to escape. And Gus—if you'd try to talk just a little—"

"Why?" asked her husband. "And what about? Shoes? No one wants to hear about my business and I've got no time for anything else, you know that."

"When Papa came to the school exercises and the principal talked to him," said Helen, "he didn't answer a single word, just nodded and then when the principal finished Papa tipped his hat and walked away."

She fixed cold, rebuking blue eyes upon him.

"What the hell," growled her father. "What do I know about education? Let him do the talking, that's his business."

"But he thought you couldn't understand English," explained Helen, flushed with shame at the recollection. "He asked Miss Murrell if you were foreign."

Gus was not disturbed. He left the table for his low leather chair in the kitchen corner, the Sunday paper in hand, lit his pipe calmly and adjusted his spectacles.

"I've got my work—let him have his," he answered.

Connie hurried to fix matters since Helen always would hang on to an argument until it was in shreds and Gus in a quiet fury.

"All right—all right, Gus, don't bother to talk to the company. But please stay at the table until they've finished eating instead of going off to the kitchen to doze right away. I would hate that, honestly, Gus."

"Don't worry about me," Gus answered impatiently. "Have your party. I can look after myself. I've never disgraced anyone yet."

"You wouldn't know it if you did," muttered Helen but subsided at an imploring look from her mother.

Miss Murrell came half an hour before the expected time. She lived with the two other high school teachers in the town's only hostelry—"The Oaks." She was seldom asked anywhere and usually was left on The Oaks' porch reading with the greatest absorption the *Atlantic Monthly* or *Harper's* while the pretty newest teacher went out driving with the town bachelor, Matt Neal, and the other in her best blue suit and white kid gloves went out for an evening of bridge (which Miss Murrell looked upon as unintellectual) with Laurie Neville or her secretary-companion, Miss Manning. Tonight she was forced to leave the house before six if her friends were to witness her departure and note that she too was sometimes invited out. They helped her into the blue crepe de chine (drapes flying from waist to neck) which Miss Neville had sent down to The Oaks for whichever of the teachers it would fit. It was almost too small for Miss Murrell but if she didn't bend her elbows it was all right.

"It's only a little supper at Mrs. Benjamin's," she explained carefully. "But Professor Decker will be there and you know how a new teacher will talk if he sees you aren't gotten up properly."

The other teachers were not envious of Mrs. Benjamin's invitation but their eyes met in mutual envy of Miss Murrell's opportunity with Decker. The only man teacher in town beside the married principal—not bad-looking and possessing a shy reserve always challenging to women even when complemented by age, gout, or stupidity. . . . In Laurie Neville's huge home one never saw a sign of a man unless it was one of her doctors from the city or the snobbish husband of some bored house guest. After Miss Murrell left the teachers looked at each other, more friendly than they had ever been.

"You know, Louise isn't bad looking, she's almost pretty, but not quite," said the young, pretty teacher, suddenly making the other young and pretty, too, with her air of including her in a secret. "Being not quite pretty is worse than being ugly, I think."

"Anyway, Louise isn't a man's woman," said the older one, and then was silent, thinking of a certain "man's woman" she had in mind who was practically wasted in Dell River.

Miss Murrell felt excited and flattered by the formal air of the Benjamin dining room due perhaps to the rigid bouquets of asters which Mimi had placed on table and cabinet. She reveled in the discomfort (always associated with high social functions) of sitting alone in a dimly lighted room waiting for the hostess to make an appropriate entrance. One imagined that soon doors would open and witty, delightful people would saunter in and talk of books, plays, poetry—talk of these things easily and charmingly instead of rolling them out like great ugly boulders into the conversation, handicaps that people of character gave themselves to conquer, no matter how painful it might be, before they could go on to the unworthy business of having a good time. Even Miss Murrell could not talk of books or poetry lightly, it was like taking out one's very heart and playing bean-bag with it. When she thought of Swinburne or of Galsworthy her head swam, blood pounded in her throat, so that she could barely speak, and when she wanted to talk in class about "Un Bel Ami" her hands shook and her eyes filled with tears, so she had to pretend to be reading from notes, and when she managed to force her words out of her trembling lips her voice was strange and harsh, so strange that pupils stared at her open-mouthed. That was what came of being shy, of caring too much for things, and of keeping them to yourself instead of getting accustomed to airing them in public.

Mrs. Benjamin, in trailing gray silk, fitted in with one's dream of a Sunday night salon. Miss Murrell felt a wave of gratitude to her for fitting in so well, she was moved further by Professor Decker in a wing collar and tie that seemed almost formal, so magnificently did he wear it, bowing over Mrs. Benjamin's hand—it was all so fitting that Miss Murrell did not mind that he merely nodded, clicking his heels, to her.

"That's why I can never be happy with simple, *good* people," she thought. "It isn't enough to be honest and good—to be happy they must pretend. They really must!"

Helen was angry because the milk curdled when she made the white sauce, so she passed the plates with a face black as a thundercloud. This was the privilege of pretty girls, they could always be rude or angry and were forgiven because tantrums accented their beauty. Mimi, tongue-tied before teachers and Helen's rage, sat at table and could not eat. She was tired of seeing everything with Helen's eyes, then with mother's, then with father's. She knew Helen resented the whole business, especially now that they were eating the soured chicken and politely saying nothing about it. Mimi knew Helen wanted to shout, "See how poor we are, we don't even have soup spoons or bread-and-butter plates, why don't you come out and say so, you teachers that have been everywhere and know the way things ought to be, you make me sick pretending not to see and not to care, talking all that rot. Come on and say what you're really thinking—that the chicken's sour, the napkins are all ragged even if you do call them serviettes!"

Mimi saw her father hurry through his portion before anyone else began, then push his plate back, and she looked quickly at her mother and the guests to see if they looked revolted. But they were laughing and talking in formal, slightly foreign accents, begging each other's pardon, thanking each other, and if-you-please-ing each other, passing their cups and dishes with elaborate ceremony, their voices quite changed with little tremors of excitement.

"They're pretending it's a party," Mimi finally decided and was awed by her discovery for she could never pretend very well, even when she was little mud-pies were mud and dolls were dolls, not babies. When she grew up perhaps everything would change and for her then Professor Decker and Miss Murrell in for supper would be a party, not just extra dishes and the strain of good manners.

Connie saw none of the things that Helen saw, she could even forgive Gus for dozing in his chair and did not mind when in the after-supper confusion Mimi and Helen started chattering about classes and wrangling excitedly not because they disagreed but because it covered their self-consciousness.

"I think we will have a little music now," said Connie, and led the way to the front room. Both ladies flushed and were happy when Decker offered his cigarette case, and each shook her head hesitantly as if on this one occasion she would deny herself. Decker sat at the piano and tried a few chords, acting as if the resulting noise were not half bad, and remarking that undoubtedly it had been a good piano once.

When he sat down the old-fashioned cut of his suit was apparent, the heavily padded shoulders, slightly raised pinched belt and the shining greenish seams. Miss Murrell watched his foot on the pedal, first because it was a small foot for a man, though he was undoubtedly no giant, and then because the tan oxfords were patched and the heels run over, and she could not help wondering how he could be so gay, quite as if he had new patent leathers on, though perhaps, she reasoned, new shoes would only have accentuated the raveling edges of his trouser cuffs. She felt guilty for taking notice of these trivial points.

"It's because I hear Marian and Stella talking so much about people," she mentally excused herself, "so I've begun to notice the things they are always on the watch for. I must stop it."

Gus had silently gone upstairs, having uttered only two words during the evening, but the guests appeared not to mind, as if the only decent way to treat such afflictions in society was to feign not to see them. In the beginning Decker had tried to talk to him but Gus had answered very briefly. Connie felt disturbed, and had a sudden passionate hatred for him, but the feeling vanished as if hatred were too big a word for such a little man. She thought of how hard Gus worked, she was moved, as always remembering that he had been left an orphan when he was only ten—ah no, she couldn't hate Gus. Certainly, if he must sleep, it was better to have him upstairs than right here where everyone could see and hear him snore.

Listening to Decker, by some magic, conjuring music out of the old tin piano, Connie grew dreamily happy. Now it seemed to her she had always led a charming life among charming people—this was not one evening in a thousand, it was the way all her evenings were spent—indeed her evening voyages of fancy were very like this reality in essence. She was about to ask Decker to play the Liebestraum but Miss Murrell did and he smiled so scornfully that Connie looked with reproach on the poor woman. Then he offered to accompany her and she sang "Come Back to Sorrento" but she had forgotten the words so she hummed the air while Decker improvised runs and trills so cleverly that she had the sensation of giving a marvelous performance. But it made her sad to think of how much she had forgotten, how much she loved music and how little she knew about it, her blind ecstasy over a mere chord made it appear irreverent to inquire what made up such rich beauty.

"I think," said Decker, "we might learn to hate music if we had to fulfill its demands. This way we can play with it, as if it were our toy. If circumstances were different—" they sighed and thought of their lost careers—"we could not play with it, for we would be its slaves."

"Yes, yes," cried Connie, happy just to hear the word "music" as women are happy to hear a lover's name mentioned.

Mimi stood in the doorway shyly listening for a while, too awed to sit down, too embarrassed to leave, conscious of her freckles, her chewed fingernails, her new budding breasts. She was afraid to speak lest she make a grammatical error before the English teacher, and she was afraid to call herself to Decker's attention lest he recognize her as the pupil he scolded yesterday for singing off-key. Presently Helen's voice, calling her from the kitchen, released her and she stayed out there pretending to do her homework on the kitchen table long after Helen had stolen out with the Herbert boy who had whistled to her from the alley.

"And do you know," Professor Decker said, "actually when I accepted the Dell River position I said to myself, 'My dear fellow, this is the end for you—you are going into the wilderness. No one will have heard of Debussy or Ravel. They will think Brahms is a disease and Mussorgsky—a mineral water!'"

Connie laughed joyously, her cheeks flushed, her eyes radiant. Miss Murrell laughed, too, and fixed the names in her mind so that in the library tomorrow she could find out if they really were mineral waters. Decker spraddled the piano stool as if he were quite at home, he looked boyish running his fingers through his thinning hair in a shy way, and he stammered a little before he said something amusing. Miss Murrell could not keep her eyes from Mrs. Benjamin who sat on the edge of the chair, her hands clasping one knee, her coral earrings quivering with each move of her head, sometimes they fell against her brown hair and sometimes against her slim, creamy throat.

"Why, she is beautiful!" thought Miss Murrell and tried to think wherein she had changed since last spring. For a moment it struck her as shocking for this woman to be a cobbler's wife—how could it have happened? And then she thought wasn't it better to be an "old maid school teacher" than to have people wondering how you came to be the wife of a cobbler or a bricklayer or a butcher, but the answer, alas, was no . . . and especially in Dell River where it was merely being decent that counted, regardless of butcher's aprons or workmen's overalls.

"It shows that everywhere—no matter where you go," Decker pursued, seriously, "you find your own people, your own kind. Isn't that true, Mrs. Benjamin?"

"Indeed it is," Connie agreed and it seemed to her that the last fifteen years had all been like this night when actually this was her first party, even the walls of her house with their old-fashioned wallpaper looked different now that they had absorbed a dozen allusions to glamorous places—"A funny thing happened to me once in Bremen. . . ." "A friend of mine in Vienna, a perfectly charming widow. . . ." (Immediately Connie and Miss Murrell blushed with pleasure as if a man who knew a "perfectly charming widow" would only associate with women he considered equally attractive so this was indirectly a nice compliment to them.) At "Of course I found Berlin at first a frightful place, simply frightful" they looked complimented again and a little benevolent as if they knew all along that Berlin was really splendid and were amused at his tourist's first impressions.

Connie felt herself swelling with joy, this lovely, lovely evening must never end—the concert pianist, the opera singer and—well, call Miss Murrell a writer, then. . . . But the evening was hers and Decker's. Miss Murrell was outside. Poor Louisa, so nearly pretty, so almost clever, what a pity not to be downright ugly rather than forever tantalized by the hairbreadth between herself and happiness. Her diluted charm made her so easy to ignore yet she was so sweet . . . too bad that with only three persons in a room you could still forget her as if she were a pale pink little ghost.

Miss Murrell kept looking at her watch. It was eleven. She would not be home till after twelve, the others would say, ah, a wild party. Her heart beat fast and her throat ached the way it did when she was about to mention poetry or her own writing. She did not know how to bring it up but she wanted to say something, to show that even if she did not understand music, she did have her divine yearnings. In a sudden pause she was so unprepared for her opportunity she could only gasp out "Swinburne" and then when they looked at her, surprised, she blurted out in a strange, breathless voice, "I mean music is like Swinburne. Like 'In a Garden.' 'Ah, God, that day should come so soon. . . .' And 'Oh Dolores, mother of pain.' So beautiful, so—so like music."

"It is beautiful!" Connie agreed and her whole body grew warm with love and sadness for the poet who could say such things.

"You know Swinburne?" Decker asked Connie, taking him away from the English teacher and giving him to his hostess. Connie nodded eagerly, for it seemed to her she did know his work, surely she did, not that it mattered, one needn't know poetry, it was only loving it that was important. Miss Murrell was reciting "In a Garden" in a dry, breathless voice, sitting upright, her face red and queer-looking, her fingers tearing her handkerchief. Connie was not conscious of never having heard this poet before, something inside her rushed out to all lovely things with a "I know! Oh, indeed I know!" The only things she really knew were the names of trees and flowers, for even in music which she loved best she had a vague superstition that exact knowledge canceled sensuous pleasure.

"I used to write poetry," said Miss Murrell, choking at her own boldness. "I only write occasionally—little essays—little— little prose poems. . . Then I teach. . . ."

"Oh yes, teaching," sighed Decker. The word seemed a disenchanting one for he looked at his watch.

"Don't go," begged Connie. "At least come in the back-garden and see what's left of my flowers. And we can look down the river."

"River's such a big name for such a little brook," Decker laughed.

Miss Murrell, suddenly sad and silent, got her hat and coat. They went out through the kitchen door and saw the dishpan piled high with their dishes and the cat reluctantly licking the remains of the soured creamed chicken. Mimi had fallen asleep over her study books, but jumped up quickly as they came out.

"Oh no, don't go out there," she begged her mother in a frightened whisper, but Connie paid no attention so there was nothing Mimi could do but follow them out, wringing her hands because everyone immediately saw Helen lying down in the backyard hammock with the Herbert boy. So, laughing as if this were quite—oh quite—usual, the two teachers said goodnight and Connie stood in the yard, watching them walk away together as if they were to be gone forever. . . . She did not say anything to Helen, who was merely angry at the intrusion, and not at all humiliated. Instead she went into the living room and closed the piano as if it were a rare old instrument whose exquisite mechanism would be easily affected by the raw night air. She started to arrange the music again and then decided to leave it the way it was. In the kitchen Mimi set to work on the dishes. Helen came in, her hair tousled, her eyes flashing, and grumbled loudly of the outrageousness of her home which wasn't a home at all where a girl had to entertain friends in a hammock instead of on a decent sofa. They clattered through the dishes together.

From the east bedroom of The Oaks the youngest teacher looked out the window, holding her nightgown over her bosom, and saw that a man was seeing Louisa Murrell home and she had the unpleasant sensation that this was a shocking insult to herself for she was the pretty teacher, the one who had beaux.

Connie went upstairs and her heart sank thinking of the episode in the backyard, almost spoiling the evening. She knew Helen was stronger-minded than she had ever been and far wiser—no use telling her of the dangers of life. What could she tell a daughter, anyway? She thought again of Tony and those summer nights. . . . As she sat on the bed, undressing in the dark so as not to waken Gus, it came to her that she had been contented then as she was tonight, and that if tonight had never happened she might never have known how utterly, completely, hideously unhappy she had been for these many years.

✧

Dell River was changed. Connie saw it now as if she were here for the first time, still not a part of it, but an amiable visitor who finds many dull places and characters delightful since she won't see them again anyway, and they heighten her complacence over her own far different life. When Mrs. Busch came to do the washing Connie no longer was disturbed at her haughtiness but smilingly indulgent. Poor quaint Mrs. Busch, she thought, and her beautiful idiot child, for that was the way Decker had spoken of them. After the girls had gone to school in the mornings she sat down to the piano and went through Mimi's "Parlor Pieces for the Piano," enchanted over a chord here and there, marking the piece in her mind so that she might speak of it later to Decker. "Don't you love that Cyril Scott thing—that one that goes this way...."

She got out her three operatic scores, "Traviata," "La Boheme" and "Martha" and hummed through them, picking out a struggling accompaniment. She thought of Decker not as a man but as the creator of a personality for herself, a beautiful role into which she gratefully stepped. No, he himself was not a person at all, but a symbol of cities, of fame, of magic. She could not think of the way he looked but of the curious way his mere presence in the town flattered her, assured her of very rare cosmopolitan qualities. Her evening fancies changed from the past and the unreal to the possible future—talks with Decker, tea on the porch or in her rock garden, serving Gus's dandelion wine when next he came to dine, making a dozen little special plans so that every day should be an event. She saw her moss-rosebush wither into its dry brown winter and was sad, then at once wanted to share this sadness with Decker. She listened carefully to the girls' tales of school, of the preparations for Christmas exercises, selections of a chorus, reports of arguments over the program.

"And what did Professor Decker say'" she would ask and if he had insisted on "Toreador" instead of "The Pilgrims' Chorus" as an opening number or an arrangement of "The Spinning Song" instead, she would nod her head in admiration of such exquisite judgment. Yes, oh yes, she could see exactly why he had decided that way....

She thought of Gus in a kind, detached way as Decker did—dear old Gus, a dear good friend of "ours".... To this point of view Gus was comfortably oblivious. Her days were arranged to lay before Decker, they became the pretty pattern of a cultured woman's life, with the window-washing, curtain-mending, cooking, marketing, as amusing little side issues of an artist's career, all quite in the category of his teaching.

When she went downtown she was always prepared with some light greeting in case she should meet him coming out of the school building or out of his apartment. Once she saw him in the music store, so after that she often went in there. Old Mills kept nothing but the prescribed pieces for young musicians, but usually a sample of the latest gramophone was on display and Connie took to playing records over and over here. For the first time she was angered at having no pocket money, she wanted to buy a record once in a while, it was so childish to have only a few pennies in her pocket, twenty-two cents for tonight's hamburger, seven cents for bread . . . nothing for "Caro Nome!" Then this very poverty became an adventure when Decker, passing by, saw her through the show-window and came inside.

"Isn't it silly that we can't buy these things?" he sighed. "I come here every day and rage that a grown-up man should have no more pocket money than a child for his candy. . . . Look at that damn instrument—only thirty or forty dollars. . . ."

"Two hundred," came Mills' voice from the desk in the corner of the store. Connie and Decker looked at each other and laughed. They started out of the shop together.

He had a slouching swagger that seemed the ideal carriage for a man of the world, and Connie wondered, when she saw men look at him a little oddly, if they were not envious of the casual jaunty way he wore his ragged clothes—shiny, greenish-blue suit with the sleeves too short, run-over patched shoes, frayed shirt, faded green necktie that was never thrust into his vest like other men's but appeared to have complete freedom to fly wherever it pleased—and that shapeless green felt hat. . . . It was provincial for a man to be neat, she decided, all very well for Gus, since it suited his German idea of system, but how charming to be above system! She knew, however, from his glances at her own costume, that it was certainly the thing for a woman to be neatly groomed.

Walking across the Square with Decker became a promenade through the Bois, they exchanged comments on the quaint design of flowerbeds, found something remarkable in the whole plan of the town, so that actually some of the most intelligent people in the world would have excellent cause to settle here.

"Sometimes I wonder," said Decker very seriously, "if a man with his own work—a writer, say, or composer—wouldn't do far better working alone in a pleasant spot like this, rather than in the confusion of Paris or New York where he is the prey of every fad, and often forced by his envy into some tawdry success."

Connie nodded in complete agreement.

"Isn't it better, I've often thought," she said, "for me to be here keeping up with my interests in music, keeping my ideals, than to have failed as an opera singer and been trapped into cheap musical comedy work?"

"Singing Red Hot Mama blues," Decker added, "with Mr. Blaine Decker accompanying you on the sax."

They laughed radiantly together, a little complacently, as if, try though they would, they could not help gloating a little over the poor souls trapped by their art, in stuffy concert halls or pitifully pretending to enjoy the hollow success of second-rate fame. Connie felt young and buoyant, a great artist taking a holiday from her public in a little quiet inland village, romping away as if she were a perfectly ordinary woman.

"I want to come and see you again some evening." They stopped at the corner of the Square. Decker stood swinging his hat, his head slightly bowed, his heels together, so sensationally chivalrous his attitude that a passing automobile slowed up and some women in the back seat leaned far out to stare. "But you ladies with your homes and your luncheons, and your teas— always so busily idle. I dare not interfere."

Connie dismissed her supposed occupation with a pretty shrug. Why didn't he drop in again Sunday—she would get in touch with Miss Murrell, too. Immediately her mind began working on plans for this "dropping in." Pimiento sandwiches, she thought, this time, and chocolate cake.

"Ah yes, little Miss Murrell," Decker said, and they both smiled indulgently, granting that she was a good little soul, no doubt unusually gifted in her quiet way, but lacking in that god-like ruthlessness so necessary to the genuine artist. By implication they granted each other this rather brutal but Olympian quality, and even while admitting that Louisa Murrell was not up to the cosmopolitan mark, they agreed to include her because she tried so hard, and things which they took as a matter of course—intelligent conversation and all that—meant so much to the poor little thing.

"I hope to have a beautiful new wardrobe to dazzle you next time," Decker promised gaily. "The good principal, Mr. Marshall, took me aside today and suggested that a new suit would enhance the dignity of my position. Something in black or blue, he thought, as if he suspected me of some Scottish plaid intentions."

They roared with appreciative laughter again, and the dreadful twenty minutes this morning was almost forgotten when Mr. Marshall, large, blue-shaven, immaculate in carefully pressed blue serge, shiny black gunmetal shoes, neat black tie, stiff white collar, had stopped Decker as he swaggered jauntily down the high-school corridor.

"Parents have commented," Marshall whispered hoarsely. "Trustees have asked me to speak of it. It doesn't look well, you know, to the taxpayers. They say on a hundred and sixty a month you really should dress better, nothing fancy, understand, just black or blue, that always looks dignified and neat—I always wear blue myself—and perhaps a fresh shirt every day. I wear a shirt two or three days myself—just fresh collars—but I notice you wear the attached collars—so—"

Decker could feel the blood swirling through his head. He, who spent an hour over bath and shave every morning, who had such irreproachable standards for grooming, even though he had to compromise on style, economize on laundry and tailor repairs. . . . As if he were a child come to the table with dirty nails! He found himself raising his hand to show that no matter what else Marshall might criticize he must surely see how impeccably manicured he was, but the ragged cuff thrust out of the frayed coat sleeve was all that Marshall's eye took in.

"A new suit wouldn't be more than thirty dollars—possibly forty, and you've just been paid," Marshall said, looking away from Decker. He hated the whole business as much as the music teacher did.

Decker would not speak of the hundred dollars a month sent to his mother. It was no one's affair but his own. When speech came back to him he found his voice, in very Oxford accents, saying, "My dear Mr. Marshall, do you know I wear nothing but linen as underwear? The very purest, the very finest linen!" Almost like a drunken man he wanted to show Marshall the London label on his underwear, the label that enabled him to swagger in any company no matter what his outward apparel might be. . . . Someone—Louisa Murrell, in fact—approached the principal, then, and Decker swung haughtily away, looking whatever pupil he passed ferociously in the eye as if no matter what that pupil may have overheard the real triumph had been his, Decker's, for he had proved that he was the true exquisite, he wore linen, pure linen next to his skin. Ten years before on his trip with Starr Donnell through Switzerland, that immortal precious summer, Starr had cast aside two suits of underwear as too small, and Decker, pretending to give them to the valet, had secretly kept them. Threadbare but elegant, he was still instructing laundresses wherever he lived in the special process necessary to the preservation of the rare fabric, storming when they were scorched or

torn, mending them himself when they fell apart. Like a magic
ring these garments kept him above all failure, all despair, they
represented foreign culture, and that year in his life when he
had been on the brink of spectacular fame. Thinking of Starr,
as he would be thinking of him forever, he knew that his heart
again seemed torn out of his body, it was impossible that two
people who were one person should be ripped apart, the only
way he could heal this anguish of remembering was by thinking hard of the perfection of that brief year, thinking of it
proudly as a triumph rather than dwelling on the end of it
which meant defeat.

How would he get a new suit, how, he thought, beating
time for "The Soldier's Chorus" that afternoon. . . . How could
he live with Marshall thinking he was a tramp, a filthy tramp
when he shaved every morning and night too sometimes,
pumiced his hands so meticulously, bathed himself, heating the
water while he dusted the apartment. Rather die than tell
Marshall that he laundered his own three shirts now to save
two dollars a month for his piano rent. Rather die than admit
anything that appeared the shoddy dreary poverty of the ordinary teacher instead of the ascetic simplicity of a true aristocrat.
Aching with shame as he had been all day, now he marvelously
recovered his dignity by chatting with Mrs. Benjamin as a gentleman to a lady.

He saw that her gloves, her black kid gloves, were to her
what the London label was to him, they made of Dell River a
center of wit and culture as a monocle and lorgnette might have
done. And when he humorously told of Marshall's suggestion,
Mrs. Benjamin's amusement made a blundering provincial ass
of Marshall, made of himself a charming but absent-minded
artist, a helpless child about fashions as all artists were, at the
same time wearing his rags with such genuine distinction that it
brought out the blind, futile envy of dubs like Marshall.

"Of course I shall forget to buy the damned suit," Decker
chuckled. "I'll buy some etching instead. There's a nice McBey

in a shop in Pittsburgh. I told the man I might send for it when
I changed cars there."

"You really are quite hopeless," Connie scolded him admir-
ingly. "I'm sure Mr. Marshall is never going to understand you.
. . . And I am quite as likely to spend the grocery money on
Caro Nome for my poor squeaky old victrola."

They laughed again and being poor became a mere youthful whim, being not quite what they once planned became a
purely temporary compromise, or at worst a philosophic adjustment which superior people made with a gallant shrug of their
shoulders.

Decker, his tie flying over one shoulder, swaggered busily
eastward, still swinging his hat in his hand and throwing his
head back as if he had an unruly mop of hair instead of not quite
enough; he continued to smile slightly, thinking of poor, stupid
old Marshall and his thirty dollar suits—as if one could get a
really decent suit such as Starr always wore for less than a
hundred. He'd rather wear these old rags than the ready-made
sort of thing men like Marshall wore. The hot shame of the
morning had vanished into a warm glow over Mrs. Benjamin,
in whose clear hazel eyes he saw himself a witty talented fellow
who found it more amusing to be a vagabond than a gentleman.
He glanced back before turning toward his doorway, and saw
her looking backward, too. She looked slim and discreet in
black, adjusting her close-fitting black velvet hat ever so slightly
to the right, her gloved hands twisting it delicately as if it were a
priceless import. A beautiful and cultured woman, Decker
pronounced her, an extraordinary woman who evidently appreciated almost to the full his own rather extraordinary gifts.
Catching each other's eye in this backward glance they experienced a sudden guilty embarrassment for each was so warmed
and stimulated by their brief intimate exchange that they almost
ignored the source of this self-gratification. Each, on second
thought, had looked back to fix in mind a clear image of this
understanding friend, and each saw the picture made up of the

actual and the desired. For years this was to be their habit, turning back a few steps after parting to fix that final image, and
always they saw the pleased smile or flush that was a tribute to
their own conversation; always Connie would be caught adjusting her hat or veil to make sure she was as soignée as Decker's
eyes had proclaimed, and always Decker would be glimpsed
twisting the end of his meager moustache in a debonair way.
Always Decker, as he did now, would bow, waving his hat with
a magnificent flourish, and always Connie, blushing a little,
would raise her little gloved hand gaily, charmingly.

꙳

Connie was not jealous when Laurie Neville invited Professor
Decker with the two teachers from The Oaks to dinner, but
Louisa Murrell suffered for her, for herself, too, since she was
not invited, and it was humiliating to have the other women
speak mockingly of Decker's mannerisms, his elegant gestures
and adopted accent warring with his ragged clothes, when she
had made so much of the privilege of consorting with the brilliant man at Mrs. Benjamin's "Sunday evenings." The other
two had been so plainly impressed all season with Louisa's private social life, the sophisticated conversations reported and the
fascinating mystery surrounding Mrs. Benjamin. Louisa had
not boasted, she could not boast, she had only referred to these
occasions as modestly as possible, but always implying their
sacredness. Miss Emmons and Miss Swasey, after their dinner
at Miss Neville's, giggled mockingly while Louisa dressed for
Mrs. Benjamin and Decker. He was so shabby, they said, and
even shabby, he needn't be such a freak, he might get a decent
haircut and some new shoes. Say what you will a man has no
business talking of the grand opera in New York and his titled
friends in Paris, the different names of wines, when he is sitting
in a lovely home with mud caked on his old shoes and his
trouser cuffs trailing raveled edges. No, now really, you could

not expect people to do more than smile at such an outrageous contrast. Laurie Neville and Miss Manning had been interested in the way they were in all freaks, but Miss Manning had assured the two teachers that he was the strangest creature she'd ever seen and pray why on earth didn't he do something about that little moustache of his—one side drooping and the other twisted up from that nervous habit of his? Why, asked Miss Manning, couldn't he direct his nervousness into twisting both ends evenly?

Louisa Murrell tried to be merely amused as she listened to them but her head swam with futile indignation that women who knew no more than the elementary subjects which they taught should be so armored in self-assurance, so certain of their superiority that they could by their smug ridicule poison the simple triumph of a really intellectual person like herself. She hated to believe that she could be even slightly influenced by their chatter. If she could only look with patronizing detachment at them as they chattered, the way, in fact, that Laurie Neville's companion looked at them if they but knew it—if she could look on with cool, faintly cynical eyes until Miss Emmons would be obliged to redden and Miss Swasey would be silent or burst out defiantly—"Well, what are you looking so superior about?" Then she would give a little embarrassed start, as Miss Manning sometimes did, and say, "Oh dear, nothing—nothing! I was only thinking how perfectly killing you two would be in a big city! Just like children disappointed to find that Bernard Shaw doesn't look like a movie idol!"

But in place of this easy annihilation *she* was the one who lowered her eyes and blushed, and made snappish defeated little retorts. No more could she silence their arguments about stories in the daily papers by saying, "Well, Professor Decker said at Mrs. Benjamin's the other night—" Miss Emmons and Miss Swasey only exchanged veiled but significant glances.

She continued to go to Mrs. Benjamin's every Sunday night, however, choking a little when she was allowed to quote poetry. Always she took along, concealed in her purse, the little album of letters she had written home from France, and sometime she hoped the moment would come when either Decker or Connie would ask if she'd brought them, and she would read them to Decker. But whenever painfully she worked up to this subject one or the other would swing it around to something else. Once Connie said, "Oh yes, Professor Decker, you should see how beautifully Louisa writes! A genuine talent! She should write novels!"

Louisa saw her opportunity then but Decker blocked it.

"By all means she should!" he exclaimed heartily. "A friend of mine in Paris is a novelist, although I've not seen any of his books recently. Starr Donnell. I remember his first novel which he wrote while we were rooming together. It's the only one I've seen published. In that he used a rather striking theme. A man, in love with his sister, actually goes through life believing he hates her, and always in his amours seeking her direct opposite—and then breaking off when a little gesture, a lift of the eyebrow, or tone of the voice, reminds him of Estelle, his sister. Now, Mrs. Benjamin, I appeal to you as a sensitive, intelligent woman, do you believe such a state of mind is possible?"

So they would talk about Starr Donnell's first novel. Louisa, instead of being angry, was secretly relieved, even in her disappointment, for those rare moments when she betrayed her secret self to anyone were frightful agony and left her shaken and weepy for days; it was such torture to bring out this self, and she was always puzzled at its occasional insistence on breaking through to the shriveling light of day.

Sometimes Decker spoke of Laurie Neville—a curious woman, he said. Why, with her money and looks, had she elected to stay in Dell River? An unhappy woman, he said, who could be so much happier in Italy or Cornwall or an Eastern city. . . . Louisa explained about Laurie's parents, her careful boarding-school training, her chaperoned world tours, her return to Dell River where all the men were too awed to

approach her, how this diffidence in men had given her a
frightful inferiority so that she could scarcely speak to a man,
feeling she was repulsive, how she went to psychoanalysts and
tried to find liberation, ended in a sanitarium one whole year,
how she had to have a nurse-companion as Miss Manning was
because she was so given to hysteria....

"Remarkable," said Decker, and Louisa's heart quickened
with pleasure that she should have contributed something to his
thoughts, for she could hear him telling about Laurie in other
cities, when he returned to his little group in Paris, he would
take Laurie's story, he would discuss it with his friend, the novelist who would put it in a book, and all this would come
indirectly from Louisa Murrell. He would even think of her as
he told it....

When Laurie Neville's invitations were for Sunday, Decker
refused them, considering Connie's invitation a standing one;
and when he went on other evenings it made his return to
Connie more flattering, and made life richer by giving Dell
River the temporary luster of a gay, social center.

Louisa did not know for many weeks that Decker served
tea to Connie alone in his apartment over the cobbler shop.
Connie had formed the habit of stopping in the shop during her
Saturday marketing. Decker was usually there, sitting on the
old oak table beside Gus' work bench, smoking cigarettes, talking constantly about Germany to Gus, who would nod his
ruddy blonde head over his work and say, "Sure . . . Sure . . .
That's right . . . Sure, I remember going to Leipzig when I was
seven years old. Visited my father's aunt. . . . A big woman, not
like the Benjamins at all. . . . A big woman with hair on her lip
like a man's and strong . . . almost break your back when she
squeezed you. I was a little fellow. Just seven. . . . And the
opera. . . . Of course . . . Tristan . . . Der Freischutz. . . . Sure, Mr.
Decker, oh sure. . . .

Connie would come in with the Sunday roast sticking out of
her market bag, and Decker would jump down from the table,

take the bag out of her hands, and they would burst into laughter at the absurdity of Connie Benjamin shopping for meat like an ordinary housewife. Gus never talked much after Connie came in, for he believed that only a ladies' man would have much to say to a woman. He let Decker do the talking, refused his invitation to drink tea upstairs while Decker played the piano, though he did accept a glass of the wine Laurie Neville had sent Decker. At six Gus went over to the Dutch barber's— Hans Feldts'—had his hair cut and beard trimmed, and he and Hans drank beer and ate leberwurst and zwiebelkuchen made by Hans' wife in the back room of the barbershop, and Gus forgot all about his wife and Decker. He was glad they did not oblige him to keep up with their constant play of talk. When, having vanquished Hans both in beer capacity and argument, he opened the shop once more, it was often eight o'clock and the upstairs windows dark. This meant that Connie had gone home to be with Mimi while Helen went out with her date, and Decker had gone, malacca stick in hand, brave in Piccadilly collar topping badly fitting suit, to Neville's or Marshall's for dinner or even to a Bridge Club supper. This was as it should be, but as time wore on Gus returned to see the light burning long after eight above his shop and heard the piano thundering, while in the shop he sometimes found the Sunday roast still lying on the work-bench, the brown paper wrapping moist with blood. And above the piano's magnificent noise Gus would hear a woman's voice sometimes singing out the words but more often humming, so that if he had not known better he would have believed it came from a violin or cello. Tying on his apron, preparing for work once more, Gus would listen a moment, frowning, he would think of the girls alone at home while their mother stayed here. Ah well, the girls were old enough to get their own supper once in a while. Decker was a harmless freak—let them make their uproar if they must. It was only once a week, like his own festivals with the German barber. So Gus shrugged his shoulders and dismissed the whole business.

♪

Professor Decker brought his servant problem to Mrs. Benjamin. Someone, he said, he needed to dust his bits of foreign bric-a-brac, to polish his samovar, and occasionally to wash his real lace dresser-scarf. Someone, he said, who knew how to handle rare things—nothing of value, of course, but all those little things one picked up traveling and could not replace in this country. The work would require two or three hours a week and Decker stated that he was prepared to pay a few cents above the average for this rather special work. Mrs. Benjamin arranged with Mrs. Busch to take on the responsibility in return for a dollar a week or two dollars if he included his two other shirts, bed linen and the linen underwear.

After that arrangement was made part of every Sunday was spent in telling amusing anecdotes about their mutual servant. She reminded Decker of the fat Felice he and his friend Starr Donnell, the novelist, had employed in Paris, though her somber pride in her half-witted daughter made him think of Marthe, the strange little old chambermaid in that Leipzig pension. Presently Mrs. Busch, all unknowing, became the rock on which innumerable layers of moss clung, upon her hinged legends about all the handmaidens of history and fiction, and her simplest word or gesture was feverishly watched so that the legend might be kept constantly alive. Mrs. Busch personally referred to Decker's effects as "trash" and hung quite as many legends upon him as he did on her, but these stories, eventually reaching Decker's ears, served as further evidence of Mrs. Busch's quaintness. Connie, at first shyly and finally quite brazenly, asked Mrs. Busch about Decker—there was not so much new that Mrs. Busch could tell her but she wanted to hear his name, hear another Dell River woman, even poor Mrs. Busch, speak with awe of his foreign background and cosmopolitan tastes until she thrilled with proud knowledge that this rare creature should come to her for understanding. Mrs.

Busch no longer had the power to make her cringe. Decker's arrival had changed that, had made of Mrs. Busch a character rather than a sinister symbol of Dell River.

Mrs. Busch sensed something amiss in the growing tender amusement of these two clients and frankly resented it, not exactly sure of what she disliked beyond the fact that this fond possessive attitude did not fit in with her idea of herself as an independent gentlewoman whose hobby was laundering. She became to Decker and Connie of more vital importance than Louisa Murrell or anyone in town for she represented that doting old retainer who figures in the background of all aristocrats. "Dear, quaint old Busch," they thought of her with tears in their eyes, gratitude for her blind, gruff devotion to their interests. Mrs. Busch regarded the two of them with profound indifference and a high measure of patronage, but everyone has the privilege of construing the attitude of others to fit in with his own philosophy.

Decker seldom called during the week, and it was on these lonely evenings, once devoted to a real and then a fancied past, that Connie thought about him. The girls would sit in the dining room, heads bent over their homework. Often Mimi studied alone for Helen was popular and free to make her own engagements. Connie sat in the porch hammock, thinking of Decker. Frost nipped off the vines, left the lattice naked, and Connie, wrapped in an old shawl, sat in the chill of early December, shivering but unconscious of discomfort, till Helen or Gus, irritated or puzzled by her queer behavior, would call her indoors.

Connie thought not so much of Decker as of herself talking to Decker, of this little childhood episode to tell him, of this opinion of Debussy to mention to him, tasting in advance his flattering amazement. One thing troubled her. Why did the image of Decker perpetually give way to the image of Tony, so that even naming the hero of her fancy "Decker" his face was unmistakably Tony's.... She seldom faced the idea of Tony but, suppressed, it raged up and down her brain, up and down, or lay in wait behind other thoughts, dark, ominous. . . . It seemed to her that she had never thought of Tony until now as a person, for when she knew him he represented only a tremendous catastrophe, so appalling that one could not analyze it, one could only accept as they came the changes it wrought, shutting doors behind one as the future dwindled down to a mere thread of day-to-day existence. Now she saw his shallow black eyes, the thick girlish lashes, the beautiful straight nose and the short muscular body as clearly as if he were before her. Each day, reluctantly she allowed herself to remember another chapter and thinking of it always in terms of conversation with Decker try to mold it into a perfectly understandable situation. If she said they had been lonely . . . if she said that no one had ever kissed her before . . . if she said that she was deliriously blind because Morini had said she might be a great singer like Melba or Patti . . . if she said they had been so much in love . . . not that they were, they were both far too carried away by their illusions of great careers . . . if she were only to say she was so young. . . .

So young. . . . In her white net graduation dress she must have looked lovely. She recalled that it had been plain, the trimming was all on the underslip, bands of pink ribbon, blue rosettes and forget-me-nots. She wore it when Manuel took her to the great man because it was her prettiest dress, and she sang "La donna è mobile—" and "Tome a Sorrento." She had told Decker of that moment, of the sudden holy feeling of being divinely selected for great deeds.

"The throat of an artist!" she remembered the exclamation and afterwards the long wait seated on a gilded Venetian chair in the vestibule while the two teachers discussed her in feverish Italian. A natural voice, but in need of training. She knew again that awed sensation of being in the hands of fate, for her voice and future seemed to be none of her concern but matters to be decided by Manuel and the great man, Driving back to her grandfather's house she had been ecstatically silent while Manuel planned for her, how he would approach her grandfather—already she was invoking those golden-mirrored salons for her future dreams. . . . Then alone at dinner with Grandfather, trying to tell him of the wonderful thing that was to happen to her, and unable to risk losing its joy by hearing his cold "Interesting! Interesting!" The story wanted to rush out but a childhood of chilling experience reminded her that it was better to keep her joy secret than to fling it to the frosty indifference of that bitter bloodless old man. Manuel would talk it over with him, but somehow she felt she must tell someone just for the telling. She was tempted to rush down the road to her old convent and tell the sisters but they were not enough, they too were indifferent. She thought of the cook but she was old and cross. Who was there to listen to a young girl telling that she was to be famous, she was to be a Jenny Lind, a Patti . . . who was there in the whole countryside to listen? Connie had wandered about the old unkept gardens of her grandfather's park, watching through the grilled iron fence the passing automobiles. She thought exultantly, "Someday they will come back here and say, 'This is where she walked the day Manuel told her. This is where she was so lonely as a young girl, seeing no one but tutors and the girls at the convent day school—no one to talk to—this is where she lived,' they will say!"

At the edge of the estate she heard sounds of a brass band. There was no night-life in the village so, curious, she walked down the lane to the town center. She had told Decker about that—how the whole village was jeweled with colored lights, a carrousel and an illuminated ferris wheel glittered through the trees. A little shy, she kept in the shadow till she came to the Square where the crowd was collected, waiting for some special performance. As Connie looked around she was jostled by a young man in a spangled tunic and white tights. "Look— there—that's Tony, the Daredevil! Look! There he goes!" She heard the whispers from the crowd about her and caught their excitement. She was glad when he turned back and smiled boldly at her. She pressed forward and saw him climb the torch-lit ladder to the balcony from which his wire stretched across to a warehouse roof on the other side of the brook. His smile had made his performance somehow her special responsibility, she blushed at the crowd's rapture. That would always be her picture of Tony—that first glamorous impression, red torch-lights illuminating a hundred upturned faces, a band playing, and high up the glittering figure of a boy in spangled lights, dancing on a silver thread. When she thought of herself singing in some great concert hall later she could not untangle the dream of her own fabulous triumph from this triumph of Tony's. Because this was the day a golden door had opened to her, Tony seemed the messenger of the gods who was to lead her into worlds of fairytale splendor. There was no explaining this in after years to anyone else—Tony himself was the only one who understood.

The Silver Daredevil had climbed down, the crowd moved on to the Sword-Swallower's tent, and Connie Greene turned slowly homeward—slowly because she knew the hurrying feet behind her were those of the glamorous dark performer, and she knew in a little while he must catch up with her. . . . Sitting in the shadow of her grandfather's hedge late that night they talked of the magical future that each saw so clearly—applause, glittering lights, the Champion Tight-rope Acrobat of the World, the greatest coloratura. Tony was eighteen, too, and in a loose tweed suit, collar open and tie carelessly knotted he was unbelievably beautiful. Perhaps she was beautiful, too, she must have been to have strangers stare so, but she had cared only for the marvel of her voice, she could scarcely remember how she looked then.

The second night she went again and saw him dancing on a huge shining ball across the wire and agonized at first with fear for him, she finally wept with joy in his arms when he came down once more.

The third day—Connie could no longer understand the utter blackness of that third day, she could weep a little in sympathy as over a daughter's grief, but understand?—that was no longer possible. She could only be grateful for the numbing process of the years. That black day after Manuel had approached her grandfather and found that his consent to her career would never be given and backing was out of the question. Even Manuel, once money was withdrawn, looked vaguely past her, promising a little sadly to do what he could. The curtain dropped on the triumph of Constance Greene—the lovely gate swung back and became a bleak door which heard no prayers, a calm, relentless door as final as her grandfather's austere brow. There was no other door for Connie, once this one closed, her world was at an end. At eighteen it was hard to believe one's world was at an end.

Dimly, in memory, she saw herself wandering to the carnival grounds that day and remembered the men packing up the Talking Doll concession just beyond the merry-go-round. She remembered the dull shock in her heart—"Tonight the carnival leaves." After the eight-o'clock performance Tony came to her and for hours they talked in that hidden hollow shadowed by the hedge. It was not important to remember, as it had been unimportant then, that they lay in each other's arms. What was important was that the gate was not closed. Tony, the Silver Messenger of the gods held it open for her, they would fly through together. She was saved.

It was hard to recall, since she had esponged it once so willingly from her mind, the girl crying alone, her cheek against the messy pine trunk, crying for sheer exultation because the miracle, after all, was to happen. Tony was to lead the way. And there was Tony running down the middle of the street to change into tights for his twelve o'clock performance. In an hour he would be back for her. She could not remember now that it was once herself, this slight girl in white stumbling across the great lawn to the house, for even then the girl had whispered, "This is where Constance Greene once lived. This is where the great singer almost stayed her days till Tony saved her, took her to New York, to a manager—"

Then an hour later, backing out of the hall door, her eyes fixed on the back of her grandfather's head—he mustn't turn, he mustn't turn and see her. Tony's hand clutching hers reassuringly in the shadow of the summer house, then flying across the lawn, speechless, to the Post Road, and waiting for the bus. One thing she could never forget, the little light of the westbound bus far, far down the road, that round, shining eye growing bigger, bigger, soon she and Tony would be swallowed in its golden immensity, her breath still caught remembering the splintering golden rays, the doorway to a new heaven. Wider and wider the glittering circle grew until she shut her eyes with a little sob, and then they were welcomed into its magic brilliance.

⚜

Seventeen years were wrapped around that Constance Greene, like rags around a mummy. Within these bandages the mummy breathed, she saw, perhaps heard, but no new pain could scar her, no new passion could stir her veins for the motif was gone, once lost in the sun no failure could touch her, no further destruction was possible. Seventeen years of kind numbness and now there was light and dark, music and silence, joy and nothing. The mummy came alive and linked today with that runaway day seventeen years ago as simply as if no dreary years came between. Connie Benjamin was Constance Greene and Tony—Tony was Decker, yet Decker was more than Tony, he was Manuel believing in her, too, and more than that he was her public. No, she decided, she could never tell Decker about Tony, even while she was preparing the way for that confession, she knew it must not be told . . . so few pretty ways of telling it, yet there it was, the final justification for her being Mrs. Benjamin of Dell River rather than Constance Greene, the singer. Her pride and sense of fitness held her back, but her desire to prove that it was fate, nothing but fate that had blocked her, was too much, and one day Decker knew.

Connie thought he might pity her, he might despise her a little as weak, but she had never dreamed that he would rage and fume like a jealous husband. He sat on the piano stool in his living room and though she had made the story quite a naive girl's idyll looked upon through later sophistication, she observed that Decker's face grew quite gray as she talked.

"You say this Italian circus performer then left you penniless, about to have a child, helpless, in this cheap hotel?" he inquired in a strange thin little voice. Connie frowned at the blunt summing up.

"Yes, but you see he was just a child himself. He hated having me or anyone dependent on him, so that instead of his being the great performer with applause, he had to be a waiter in a restaurant, just to keep us both alive. Oh, you can understand that. When the chance came he had to run away with the show again. Don't you see? He had to?"

Decker shut his eyes and leaned his head on his hand.

"I can't. No. . . He promised you an introduction to this singer who was to help you get started— "

"It wasn't his fault the man wasn't in New York, and he was too young, too gay to be bothered with marrying. He wasn't the type," Connie protested.

"He left you half-starving for days! I understand why you couldn't go back to your grandfather's. But that you, a delicate, gentle girl—an artist—"

As he spoke Connie felt the stab of that old anguish. . . . Day after day watching from behind the torn lace curtain in the Atlantic City hotel, watching for Tony to come back, the heavy ache of her own body, her heart a dull metronome of pain, ticking out the days till doom came. She shivered remembering

with awful clearness the days walking up and down the Board
Walk, huddled in his discarded overcoat, her mind dulled to
everything but the thundering of the waves. Who was she, why
was she here, what was to happen to her, these things were lost
in the rhythmic beat of the sea, but back in the dreary little
room, waiting behind the lace curtains—A drowning person,
Connie suddenly snatched Decker's hand.

"But then Gus came, don't you see? Quite out of the blue
this perfect stranger came and took me away. I'd never dared
even hope for such a thing but he came—don't you see how
splendidly it all worked out? Even if I did lose the baby—who
but Gus would have been so kind, no one but a simple, good
person like Gus would have tried to talk to me and seen at once
what was to be done...."

"It's outrageous!" Decker cried out. "I could kill that circus
ape. Connie, how dared you be so weak, so common, as to go
away with him? How could you do it? I hate it, I wish I'd never
known. Why tell me now?"

"But we've told each other everything else," Connie said
faintly. She was frightened now for they were losing Decker,
the cultivated stranger, and Mrs. Benjamin, that delightful
artist, in a mere man and woman; she couldn't bear to feel them
slipping into these simple, ordinary molds. "I went with him
because he was mixed up in my mind with my career, my
future—don't you see?"

"Ah, you were crazy about him!" Decker shouted at her.
His hands gripped the piano bench, and she couldn't help seeing that for a pianist they were such small hands. A lock of hair
dropped over one eye, his mouth quivered, and Connie was
shocked that he did not seem conscious of this lack of poise.
"You were like any other woman when a big brawny brute
came along ... why tell me? Why tell me about it at all?"

His fist beat the keyboard unexpectedly and a thunder of
bass chords roared support. Connie saw that for some reason it
had been a mistake to tell him. She heard the water boiling in

the samovar for the tea and she glanced regretfully at the two china cups waiting to be filled, but now she could not stay.

"Well—say something, go on, tell me of this deathless love of yours," Decker challenged her, trying to control the break in his voice. "Tony the Daredevil. Go on, let's hear more of the little idyll."

"There's nothing more to say," Connie said dully. She was putting on her hat. She didn't look at him, for fear the picture of an angry, blazing-eyed little man would insidiously replace the other portrait of the suave, poised man of the world. She knew he was looking at her accusingly, waiting for her to say more but it was quite true she had nothing to say. You can not talk about real things, there are no words for genuine despair, there are not even tears, there is only a heavenly numbness for which to pray and upon that gray curtain words may dance as words were intended to do, fans and pretty masks put up to shield the heart.

So Connie did not want to look at Decker now, unshielded, nor, since he was tearing down her own curtain, dared she remain; without their words between them she was frightened. She saw her sad but rather charming story of young love ripped down to its grim skeleton—betrayal, hunger, bleak agony—this was not what she had wanted Decker to see, this was not what she had wanted to remember. It was amazing to find that no matter how well she had dressed the facts the bones of tragedy still emerged, and she, as its heroine, became a weak little object of common pity, an ordinary human being, not Mrs. Benjamin, the artist, just as Decker had changed into a jealous, ineffectual little man, with the glamour of foreign places receding from him ever so gently, leaving what might have been the real man but a stranger to Connie, a stranger who was marring a structure built with infinite care. She went to the door, not allowing herself to think or to face the destruction he was wreaking in their design, not daring to wonder if this was the end, if their little game of words could ever be caught up again.

Decker watched her, his eyes glassy, as if he were drunk, Connie thought, and when she put her hand on the doorknob, his voice, shrill and cracked like an old man's came to her—

"Like any other woman, falling for the first big truck-driver that comes along, not caring about anything else. Music—bah—it was nothing for you but something to mark time till a lover came." He tried to make his breathing more even so that his words would have the power of restraint. Automatically he picked up the purse Connie had dropped and handed it to her, the habit of chivalry was stronger than anger, for struggle though he would against the impulse, he could not help holding her coat for her the next minute.

"Women put no value on themselves—no matter how cheaply you hold them they themselves would sell for less, and you—that you, of all women. . . ." Connie silently buttoned her coat and he opened the door for her, clicking his heels in his farewell bow as if his body with its training in polite gestures were at the command of someone else, operating smoothly, while he, quite apart, led an independent, undisciplined life. Still Connie did not want to look at him, she could not bear to lose any more than she had already lost and she could feel it slipping from her, the precious conviction that her life had been a charming one, the anguish and despair of eighteen was before her again and the sudden complete horror of seventeen blank years. She couldn't bear to lose what he had given her, better to blunt every other feeling, even pride, than to lose that lately won faith in a pretty destiny, so Connie pulled her forces together and threw out both hands in an operatic gesture of res-ignation.

"What is one to do with so much temperament? It shows the artist isn't quite dead, doesn't it, for us to scream like two children at each other," she tried to smile into his white angry face. "I can't stay another minute or we'll be actually quarreling —you and I of all people—quite as if we were Dell River itself—" She managed quite a gay little peal of laughter and drew gloves on her trembling hands, adjusted the little veil on her hat—with gloves and a veil it was easier.

She held the laugh till one foot was on the stairs and chattered in a light trembling voice as she went downstairs, one hand groping the banister, her eyes straight ahead. "I'm afraid that Mozart you heard at Miss Neville's this afternoon unstrung your nerves, the way it always does me. My teacher used to tell me that Mozart was soothing—" Her voice shook and she dared not look back—"but you know I agree with you, perfection can be as disturbing to civilized persons like us as primitive music. I—I never liked primitive things. Those Oriental songs, and those African motifs—they leave me—quite cold. Some people—some people—" she was on the last step now and she was saved, her creation of a Mrs. Benjamin was saved—"some people prefer them—"

"Constance!" He hadn't meant to call her but her name slipped out. She looked up quickly and saw him, clinging to the side of the door, weak and spent and gray.

"We'll have tea some other day," she said, her voice bright and convincing, "very soon, Blaine."

The vestibule door closed softly, she must have gone straight into the street without waiting for Gus in the shop. Decker stumbled back into the room, brushed his hand over his eyes and dropped into the chair by his desk. He sat still and dazed for a long time until his body slumped gently forward and he spread his two hands over his face, covered his burning closed eyes.

"Starr!" he groaned. "Oh my dear Starr, where are you now?"

☙

They dared not see each other for Decker could not recapture the enchantment. He knew this, puzzled over it constantly, why had he set out to break this delicate thread, knowing well enough how little it could bear. . . . Perhaps for the same reason a child deliberately breaks a rare vase, merely to end that intolerable fear of breaking it.

But, if this was finished, what was there left in Dell River? Without Connie to hear his interpretation of life it became a poor teacher's dull routine in a dull village. Laurie Neville's occasional musicales were no longer, as they appeared in properly described retrospect, gay cosmopolitan events but amateur programs by third-rate musicians, the frantic efforts of a neurotic lonely heiress to warm up her bleak life. Teaching selected groups in high-school the "Soldiers' Chorus," or "Toreador," was of itself dreary mockery. He met Louisa Murrell in the gloomy corridors every morning and thought, "The day may come when I'll think I'm no more brilliant or extraordinary than she is. I may think I fit in here as well as she does." Thoughts, which up to this time, had arranged themselves in the shape they were to be presented to Mrs. Benjamin, in little bouquets of wit and philosophy, grew morbid and self-flagellating with no destination in view. Memories, even memories of Starr, were dangerous under their dust, one needed an eager audience before a delightfully impersonal patina could be attained for them and the flavor of elegance put into one's past. The artist's and gentleman's past which Connie Benjamin had invoked for Decker could not support him without her constant encouragement. His shoulders drooped a little. Louisa, watching him from the girl's cloakroom as he strode down the corridor, observed the disappearance of the swagger, and wondered if Mr. Marshall had spoken to him about the way he walked, or worse, if he'd at last noticed the students imitating him on the streets.

But he couldn't see Connie yet, he had to be quite sure he could command the old casualness, he had to be certain tears would not come to his eyes as if he were some Dell River farmer, thinking of a young girl's trouble eighteen years ago, thinking of Mrs. Benjamin as a crippled human soul instead of a gratifying impersonal invention. The habits of walking down certain streets at certain times, harmless little tricks for meeting each other unexpectedly now had to be abandoned, though every moment one ached at the loss. In Decker's mind this unfortunate afternoon with Connie grew inevitably into the memory of his last afternoon with Starr Donnell. Each time he had desolately seen himself destroying the thing he loved, powerless to control himself, watching himself air a burst of pride or small vanity at the risk of his whole life. That hotel room in Geneva . . . the unconquerable feeling that he must be recognized as Starr's equal, Starr must know he was a person, but why? Hadn't he had a glorious year worshipping, adoring Starr, happy in sheer proximity to such a dazzling richly favored figure? Was it not compliment enough that he, of all people, should be Starr's preferred companion and confidant—he had been flattered many times in Paris and on the Mediterranean steamer when whispers reached him, "That's the friend of Starr Donnell, the writer. They say his name is Decker." Why should this same whisper suddenly enrage him so that he must assail Starr with unforgettable insults, break irrevocably the thing between them? Content, nay flattered to be the slave for so long, the moment came when the position infuriated him, the pride in his own talents which Starr's flattering friendship had created must needs overreach itself and repudiate the very relationship that had inspired it. There was no place in Starr's life for an equal and no adjustment was possible after the roles of master and slave had once been assigned. Decker had known this was the end even while he was denouncing Starr. He knew, as one committing suicide must know, that this was final. Yet they could not withdraw the rare intimate things they had given each other, they could not—once having bared every vanity to each other—look each other in the eye and deny their so generously confessed weaknesses. What demon of self-destruction had seized him then as it had with Connie . . . it had been the end so far as Starr was concerned; how could it fail to be final this time?

He found himself hurrying past the cobbler's door, starting like a guilty lover when Gus called to him, avoiding his eyes as if actually he had some secret to hide. In the school auditorium, waving his baton for sophomore girls to sing "The Spinning Song" his preoccupied glance would suddenly fall on Helen Benjamin and he would be faint with nostalgia for the old self-assurance, his cheeks would redden and girls in the front row would nudge each other and look slyly around to see if Miss Murrell had come in the room for this was the romance Dell River had invented for him.

By some miracle the two did not meet each other for an entire week, but when Sunday night came Decker knew that another week could not pass like this, no matter in what state he went back to the Benjamin house, go he must. There was no use waiting for a return of the old easy manner, that would come after the meeting, not before. He could not beg forgiveness, he only hoped she would pretend to forget. Brooding with shame over his own hysteria he never thought of Connie's possible reaction to the scene.

Where had she lost their thread, Connie puzzled, lying in bed beside Gus' heavy, sleeping figure, at what exact instant had the amused deference in Decker's blue eyes changed to curious suspicion, then to angry accusation? How blind she had been to miss that turning point when balance was within saving. . . . She had said—what? . . . Again in sharp detail Tony was invoked, she tried to recall just what words she had used concerning him to make her few months with Tony appear such a degradation. She could not for the life of her remember, yet she dared not analyze too well lest she come upon some naked reason more perilous to face than this bewilderment. What had she said, or was it some way she had looked?

Sunday without Decker was intolerable, as if the week were lost without this bright marker. She could not get out of bed, she seemed actually ill all day and Mimi brought her a breakfast tray, delighted to display her training in Domestic

Science. Late in the afternoon, with no one to look forward to seeing, a frightened feeling of deprivation came over her. She looked out of her bedroom window and saw behind the seared garden hedge the thin rusty trickle of Dell River now laid bare by the lost foliage on either bank. Beyond this creek a series of hills swelled out past the town border to farmland and far-off woods. Connie closed her eyes as if this were a dreary nightmare today, though often she and Decker had commented with pleasure on the mysterious shadows on these hills. The street, too, depressed her, viewed through the opposite window, even though at this hour it was brightened with little strolling groups of citizens in Sunday clothes, families crowded into automobile back-seats. Where would Decker go today—to Laurie Neville's perhaps or to a bridge party in The Oaks' living-room? Languidly she dressed and trying not to think of Decker or the aching present, found herself thinking of Tony. She knew that in some curious way they represented one and the same thing to her, a belief perhaps in the Constance Greene legend that she had herself created.

Where was Tony? A little fearfully she examined details of his desertion, permitted herself to remember the soiled, elaborate red silk scarf he left behind, the half-used bottle of hair pomade on the dresser, yes even the torn Irish crochet bureau-runner and the deck of gilt-edge playing cards with the dark girl's rosy face printed on the backs. Connie saw the cards again scattered over the red-flowered carpet, a dozen girls with left shoulder bared, forever smiling with a champagne glass lifted to their lips, all the little things that made her wait one day more and one day more in spite of Gus' blunt advice, for surely Tony, wherever he was, was incomplete without his cards, his loosely knotted red scarf, his violet pomade. . . .

Afraid for so many years to think of these things Connie now sought them out as protection, for the thought of Decker was an uncovered live wire, too dangerous to approach unequipped. At last she could think of Tony and wonder if there had been more real love in that adventure than she had hitherto guessed. Thoughtfully she pulled on a kimono and went up to the attic. Downstairs Gus fidgeted, waiting for supper, afraid to voice his increasing hunger lest his wife be ill in earnest—occasionally he went to the hall door and called upstairs, "Connie! Say—say Connie!" and when no answer came he would glance frowning at his watch—6 — 6:30 — 6:45.

In the attic the candles could no longer cope with the increasing darkness and Connie got up stiffly from the floor by the trunk. She was too tired now to put back all these old relics, the dress in which she'd run away, the program of "Louise" which Manuel had taken her to hear the day before her audition. She carried downstairs to her bureau drawer the pictures of Tony in tights, the red scarf, moth-eaten and frayed, and the two clippings she had put in the *Billboard*.

"Tony: Waiting for you in same place. C.— "

Waiting too long, Gus had said. Doing her hair Connie stopped to look at the pictures again. She remembered the landlady had recommended the *Billboard* as the only way to reach him. She thought of him after she went downstairs, through the girls' conversation, she thought of him all night and the next day, putting him together once again with a hundred tiny pieces until the shadow of Tony, complete, had almost obliterated Decker and had filled the barren hills of her exile with a rich warming glow. Afraid to lose this protecting image she barely spoke to anyone but held it fast, a golden shield. The next night she sent a notice to be published in the *Billboard*:

"Tony: C. wants to hear from you again after
eighteen years. No. 672 Billboard."

She was frightened after she'd sent it, but she could think of what might come of it, and she wanted to be prepared with thoughts in case Decker should slip out of her life.

✌

Days dropped in the wastebasket, blank pages from a meaningless calendar. Connie saw nothing before them, nothing following. She heard her voice discussing market errands with Helen and arithmetic with Mimi, and wondered curiously what divinity operated these superficial motions of a person after the essence had vanished. No word came from Tony and she realized she had neither expected it nor been prepared for any further step had news come from him. It was Decker's notion that Tony had been the great thing in her life, she had never thought of him as anything but a means of escape, nor had she ever reproached him in memory for being jailer rather than liberator.

Mrs. Busch came in and must talk of Professor Decker until Connie was desperate, trying to devise some means of mending their broken chain. Helen told of the boys mocking Decker's clipped, precise English, and Gus commented on a certain strangeness in his tenant's manner of late. Even the most disparaging news of him excited Connie. The children telling her he was mocked, Mrs. Busch questioning his sanity made her think proudly, "Everyone talks about him—in less than a year he's made himself a unique figure in this neighborhood. No wonder he is so important to me—he is to everyone." On the second Saturday Connie found herself in the music store watching the street cautiously from time to time to see if he would pass. She could not face a second Sunday without him, for even her thoughts of Tony were empty with no audience to hear them translated into fascinating revelations. In her mind she repeated over and over what she would say if Decker should appear. "Decker, my dear! How nice to run into you again. I've been meaning to drop you a note but you know how busy we housewives are!"

She saw Laurie Neville's car drive up and Laurie, in a great bearskin coat that made her sharp handsome face look pinched and hungry, got out with her efficient tweed-garbed companion. She heard them call out Decker's name and saw him hurrying across the street. He looked strangely little and cold in his badly fitting suit with no overcoat, yet he would not of course betray himself by pulling up his collar. Connie kept her back to the window and her lips moved in repetition of her lines. The shop door opened.

"But I never wear an overcoat—never!" Decker was protesting. "It's such a nuisance, really. I have to have one on hand, of course, but I'm always forgetting it, so why bother with one?"

"But don't you freeze?" Miss Neville begged to know.

"I love the winter," Decker answered. "I never feel the cold." He saw Connie.

"Decker—my dear!" she put out her left hand casually as if her right were far too busy fingering the records. "How nice to run into you. I've been meaning to drop you a note—"

"Oh you busy women!" he interrupted, shrugging his shoulders in despair. "It's a marvel to me you have any time at all for us poor unfortunate males. . . . What are you buying now, you extravagant creature? Not that Schumann Concerto!"

"Just wishing for it," Connie said.

Laurie picked up the book containing the Concerto and then put it quickly down, not daring to buy it before someone who confessed not being able to buy it.

"Perhaps Mrs. Benjamin can come to your Sunday evening," Miss Manning said quite clearly to Laurie. "It's next Sunday and there'll be music—some musicians on their way to Detroit. Can you come?"

"She must come," Decker said. (They were getting back again, he thought, but did not dare exult too soon.) "Old Gus, too, and perhaps the girls."

"I'll try to come," Connie said brightly as if she would have to consult a crowded engagement book first. Then she lowered her head smilingly to all of them and started out. Decker leapt to the door, held it open with almost reverent courtesy. She nodded, smiling to him, and carrying herself as one accustomed to having all doors held open and canopies thrown up for her. They had achieved the right tone once more, he thought joyously, hastening back to Miss Neville and Miss Manning.

"A sweet woman," said Miss Manning, looking out the window rather curiously after the vanishing figure.

"Charming!" declared Decker and squinted down his cigarette as if thus to find a more exact word for his description. "Yes, a thoroughly charming person!"

⌇

It could not be helped, Decker finally decided, pacing up and down his living-room, smoking furiously, and conscious of himself as a man with a dilemma pacing and smoking as if he were Lou Tellegen or John Barrymore. This idea made the dilemma itself bearable. Here it was January and here was he with no overcoat, croaking and sneezing, calling for "Doreador" and "The Sbidding Zong" which young fools of course loved to mock. Croaking and shivering, not even daring to wear his raincoat, a plain confession of poverty, and sounding insanely ridiculous when he barked out his explanation, "No, I never wear an overcoat. I never feel the cold. Hot weather—ah, then's when I suffer—" winding up this remark invariably with such a fit of sneezing and whooping that people stared as if he were mad. Well, he probably was. At this point, lighting a fresh cigarette, he saw himself as the mad genius, tearing his hair and muttering to himself. The mad music-master.

But if he used next month's salary for a coat then he could not send his mother the money for her three weeks down South. Which was the worse pain, shivering before Dell River, or confessing to his mother that quite as she suspected all these years, he was incompetent. . . . Even before he put it into words Decker knew which of these two situations he could never meet, even without pausing to look at his mother's handsome superior face, without remembering her letter—"Everyone's going down to St. Augustine again. These women who have broker-sons! (Stupid creatures of course with no more notion of who your Debussy is than I myself have, but they do appreciate how dreary middle Massachusetts is in winter.) I sometimes wonder, Blaine, if I didn't emphasize the artistic too much in your childhood, encouraging you and perhaps forcing you beyond your real capacity in music. It was only because you did so poorly in school, dear, and I was so glad to find something in which you could excel. Anyway, it's all too late now and I'm willing to say it's much my fault. Your town sounds beautiful and your apartment so luxurious that I look on my own modest cottage with great discontent. However, one must make the best of things. Certainly I shall loathe the place during February when Alma Trent and Mrs. Ford are in the South. . . ."

He could see the crisp note he would write, ignoring her challenge, enclosing his check for $100 and at the same time confessing that he meant to make it more but new suits, coats and all the paraphernalia that his rather amazing social position here required forced him to be niggardly. Much better that she should accuse him of selfishness and extravagance than of incompetence or failure. . . . Much better that he should teach Dell River to sing America through their noses, sneezing every measure, than that his mother should say, "It's quite all right. I never expected you to succeed anyway, dear boy." A wave of violent hate came over him, thinking of her lovely cold face, her correct mouth, her faint violet perfume—he saw the bottle on her bare dressing-table, the same violet essence, expensive— (one drop on her handkerchief was enough) from the same parfumeur every year at Christmas as far back as he could remember. The rage passed as it always did leaving him depressed, with the certainty that nothing, nothing would ever erase the faint contempt from that mouth, no sudden expression of admiration would ever be surprised in those eyes. She knew her son very well, was devoted to him as wives are sometimes devoted to their husbands as inadequate, futile blow-hards whose occasional triumphs prove not superior wit but fool's luck. But his brother Rod—ah that was another matter. He could lie and cheat and bully his mother and draw nothing but a soft, fatuous smile of adoration. Why Rod had only to rumple her hair and she was ready to give him the world—take away Blaine's share if necessary, but darling Rod must not suffer. Decker's fist clenched remembering how many, many years this jealousy had nagged at him, even after all these years of absence from both of them the pain of thinking of their understanding glances could still draw childish tears to his eyes.

So he must write the note to his mother, possibly even the score by some patronizing question as to whether Rod was on his feet yet or still loafing on his rich wife's money. To inflict that hurt would ease his own a little.

But nights in Dell River were frigid in January, once chilled no fire could thaw you out and Decker could see himself calling on Mrs. Benjamin next week (for that was understood once more) paying his compliments to her and Louisa Murrell with nose blue and teeth chattering. And Laurie Neville's musicale next Sunday night, the function of the season, you might say, for Dell River. He would arrive wet to the skin with snow—of course it would be a blizzard—the colors of his best tie would be damply running over his best shirt, and he would be wheezing like a steam calliope. They would ask him to play accompaniments for Miss Manning to sing her little Weckerlin songs and his fingers would be so stiff that he would fumble and how impossible his wet, mussed suit would look there at the piano. . . . Marshall, blue-shaven, immaculately dressed as befitted a school principal, would be watching him, taking it all in.

Decker, thinking of Marshall's cold gray eyes, weakened a little, then his glance fell once more on his mother's picture and he sat down to his desk. Winter—Laurie Neville's Sunday evening—Mr. Marshall—all these things would pass (in his mind he jumped lightly into April)—but his mother's cynical smile was fixed, all other struggles must be abandoned for combatting this permanent foe.

It frightened him a little, as miraculous demonstrations are bound to do, when leaving the house to mail his note to Mrs. Elsie Decker, Shaler, Mass., he encountered Marshall outside the shop door hunting for a bell.

"Oh hello, Decker—there doesn't seem to be any way of getting in here."

"There's no bell," Decker said a little coldly, sensing the implied criticism of his living-quarters. "After Benjamin goes at night you call out or throw something against my window and I have to come down."

"Rather complicated," said Marshall. He avoided Decker's eyes guiltily and—after taking in the other's light clothing—he pulled his own coat up under his chin securely. "Unless of course you don't want guests."

"I enjoy company," Decker answered. "I have always entertained constantly until—of course—this year. In the towns I've taught I used to take a huge place and have my evenings regularly."

Then he saw that the reason Marshall was embarrassed was that he was carrying a huge box, its string and tissue paper trailing on the frosted sidewalk, and he knew at once that this was a coat for him. He knew, too, that they would have to talk about a dozen other things before they got to winter, colds, and overcoats, and both would get more and more confused every minute until finally Marshall would blurt out something like, "Oh by the way, Decker, speaking of the Easter exercises, here's an old coat you can have." And he would have to be amazed and say, "Coat? Coat? Oh yes, coat—why so it is. Of course I never wear one but as a favor to you I may accept. . . ." No sooner had Decker recognized the principal's mission than Marshall saw that he did, so they stood under the dim street lamp looking uncertainly at each other, Marshall trying to hide his enormous parcel and at the same time indignant that Decker should make him feel like an ass instead of the benevolent overlord he fancied himself. Decker sailed into the silence, waving the letter to his mother, chattering of her winters down South, of her beautiful home just outside (by 200 miles) of Boston.

"He might at least ask me inside," Marshall thought angrily while Decker with shaking fingers tried to light a cigarette in the gently falling snow since a cigarette always gave him opportunity for grand gestures. He was warmed already by the prospective coat, and saw himself swaggering past Marshall in it, making vague mention of his English tailors and almost forgetting that the swaggering could not be done safely before the donor. He wanted to rush down to Connie Benjamin's house at once and show her the coat, show her the beautiful stitching, speak of the excellent work on the lining as a connoisseur of tailoring would speak. It didn't matter that the coat wasn't his yet or that he hadn't seen it. But finally Marshall shoved the box at him.

"It's not mine, really—it belonged to my wife's brother, but since you haven't got yours yet and you're about the same size as George Almon—"

"I wish I could use it but I never wear a coat," Decker heard himself saying, "of course in a storm I might, but I use one so seldom it's hardly worth while taking it. However I will keep it—thanks, of course—as a matter of fact I'd already sent to my tailors in London—on Bond Street, you know. I instructed them to send samples and I sent my measurements, of course it's terribly expensive but I don't believe in sparing a cent when you're after the best tailor—but then there's the delay—and the mails went astray—in fact my order only reached them a few days ago—I can cable a cancellation —"

"A cable's expensive, too," said Marshall, stamping his feet partly because they were slowly freezing and again because he hated Decker and his sudden change to a British accent, and he wished he could take the coat back and rush to his own fireside with a to hell with you and your fine tailors, go on and freeze to death.

"Only a few dollars," Decker smiled and went on wildly— now he was clutching the box with one arm. "I was just writing my mother to send me a few of my old winter coats that I left in her attic. Among them I should find one or two adequate—"

"I thought you never wore them," roared Marshall, unable to bear more.

"I don't—or seldom do," Decker answered quickly. "But one always has a coat of course, wearing it or not. As a matter of fact I've never been satisfied with any of them since I had my Scotch woven ulster, the one I wore tramping through Brittany. The work on that coat! The sheer beauty of its workmanship— actually, Marshall—"

"If you're getting all these other coats, then give this one back for God's sake," Marshall wanted to say but instead he only growled, "Yes, of course. Then you don't want this one?"

Want it? Decker was crushed for a moment.

"Oh, I can find some use for it," he said limply, and then, his arms clutching the package, he dropped his letter in the mailbox on the lamppost and started back toward the house.

"Won't you come up, Marshall?" he asked rather patronizingly. "I could give you a little touch of wine, or tea if you prefer?"

"No," grunted Marshall. Decker felt a jarring note somewhere. He wanted to say something light and casual to show that he saw the quaint humor of one gentleman presenting another (and that other Blaine Decker of all people) with a coat, but something rather ominous in Marshall's eye restrained him. He hesitated in the doorway.

"Then goodnight, Marshall, old chap," he called out genially, for merely holding the coat gave him the advantage

over Marshall. Good old Marshall, he thought, stupid, blundering, well-meaning old Marshall, so puzzled and yet underneath
it all so unquestionably impressed by the brilliant savoir-faire of
his music-teacher.

"Poor old boy." Decker, back in his room, tipped up the
lamp-shade to examine his new coat. A chocolate brown wool
with padded shoulders and pinched back and extra buttons,
slightly worn at the elbows and a tiny patch under the arm.
Decker tried it on and having nothing but a shaving mirror
held this at different angles before and behind him to get the
effect.

"Not bad, not bad at all," he murmured. "A little snappy,
but fortunately I can carry that off. . . ."

Poor, stuffy old Marshall. He must do something for him
sometime, show him that he didn't look down on him just
because he was a small-town school principal. Yes, he must do
something for the poor old boy.

⤳

Mimi thought about her mother when she went to bed every
night. It was pleasant when one knew one was plain and dull
and would very likely be a plain dull old maid for everyone
prophesied this, to know that one's mother at least had been
beautiful and glamorous, that one's mother from infancy on
had walked in an enchanted path, and one could cling to this
victory of one's own blood at least. Mimi thought about her
mother's near-career until it became real, for hundreds of
nights she had continued in her mind a story of unending triumph for her mother. She shut her eyes and the pictures
obediently unwound before her, her mother beautiful as the
dawn in shining white satin and a golden halo receiving ova-
tions before a red plush curtain, bowing this way and that. The
picture varied only as Mimi changed the costume from white
satin to delirious blue jewel-studded velvet, and the setting

from a stage to an enormous drawing room like Miss Neville s only ten times as large. Gentlemen resembling Blaine Decker in opera hats and tail-coats kissed the beautiful creature's hand and threw bouquets of fabulous roses at her. This was Mimi's private life, an imaginary spectator of her mother's imaginary career. Imagination stopped here, it could perform no such miracles for Mimi herself. Present or future she saw only the facts of her plain, stout little body, her slow anxious brain, stolidly she accepted her limitations, even in fancy she could not make herself a heroine. Boys ignored her, though sometimes at birthday parties one rejected by Helen would take Mimi home just to be near the sister, and Mimi, knowing this, would be tongue-tied. They would walk from the party to the Benjamins' very door without Mimi being able to utter a word. Her escort would carry on a conversation with Helen and her preferred companion walking in front of them, and at the door Mimi would scuttle inside, leaving Helen to say the goodnights.

Mimi's feeling toward Helen who was complacent with beauty and shrewdness that passed for brains was not envy but astonishment and alarm. In the main girls' cloak room Mimi stood twisting her handkerchief in a dull hopeless panic while Helen urged a little duster of girls to cut the physics class until the teacher gave up her new system of weekly examinations. Helen played truant with Bessie Herbert and they went skating on the pond by the Nurseries.

"But what will you do if Mr. Marshall finds out you weren't sick—if someone at the Nurseries tells on you?" Mimi whispered anxiously when Helen told her that night.

Helen shrugged her pretty shoulders. "He can't do more than kick us out."

"Expel you? Oh, but Helen, if he really should expel you—"

"I wouldn't care," Helen declared calmly. She was undressing before the mirror, pausing occasionally to study herself critically with infinite appreciation. "I'd like to know what good all that bunk is anyway, especially if a person's going on the stage the way I intend to do. Believe me, I'd get out of that old school as fast as they would let me—glad of the chance. I'd go straight to New York or maybe to Hollywood and go straight on the stage."

"You wouldn't have the money!" Mimi's heart was thumping furiously. She was ready to cry at the mere thought of the disturbance Helen was planning.

"I'd get it out of Papa. He's got some salted away, the old tight-wad. I heard the boys talking about him once and they said he had money, he was an old miser, they said." The idea had evidently held Helen. "Miser, mind you. Can you beat that? With us wearing the same winter coats the third year running. . . . You bet I'd get out of this place if I got a chance. Let old Marshall expel us. I don't care. Bessie might mind but I wouldn't."

"It would be awful for Mama," Mimi reminded her. "Mama wouldn't know what to do. And with Miss Murrell and Professor Decker always coming here, they'd talk about it and Mama would just die!"

Helen braided her hair in two thick bronze braids and then sat on the edge of the bed in her white cotton nightgown polishing her fingernails. Mimi, lying in bed, watched her, aghast at her and eternally puzzled. How did Helen think of these wonderful things to want, for instance, why should she—any more than Mimi—be gifted with such fierce desires for silk underwear, a sequin evening dress, ocean voyages, a stage career—and why should it be such rotten injustice for her to be deprived of these things? After all, none of the other Dell River girls had them or even felt entitled to them. Mimi tried to reason this out but found no answer. Helen was the victim of a terrible conspiracy, there was no use arguing about it or even consoling her, and, above all, it was futile to compare Helen's lot with her own or any other ordinary girl's, since it must be distinctly understood that Helen was ineffably superior and the service she had done the humble Benjamins

years ago in allowing herself to be born to them instead of to
the great families she might have selected was a favor that
should be properly paid for.

"Mama's got no right to talk to me about what I do," Helen
went on—she rather enjoyed and was whipped to further defiant attitudes by Mimi's wide alarmed eyes. "Just because she
was a failure is no reason I should be. She can't stop me. Dad
can't stop me. If I want to be something they can't stand in my
way. What'd they ever do for me? Might as well be an orphan.
No clothes—no pocket money—I can't even have my own
room, but have to sleep with my kid sister."

Mimi said nothing though she thought vaguely that Helen
had a rather crushing way of listing her injustices. Helen pulled
out the chain of the blue-shaded lamp and yanked up the window. She got into bed and lay tensely beside Mimi.

"Mama!" she repeated the name scornfully. I'd like to just
hear her try to talk to me. I'd like her to try just once."

She gave a bitter little laugh.

"One of these days I'm going to jump in and tell her just
what I've been thinking all these years."

"Oh Helen!" Mimi pleaded in a little gasp.

"You wait," said Helen. "Just you wait."

⁂

Louisa Murrell knew that the other teachers at The Oaks
thought Professor Decker was her suitor, and therefore it hurt
all the more to know it was not so. She was not in love with him
but one has to have something, and Decker was the only
strange man in town, the only man she saw outside school
except when she went to Mr. and Mrs. Marshall's and the principal, though handsome enough in his way, was not really a
man; he was a husband and a school. Decker was, on the other
hand, culture. He was also eligible. Like most women, married
or single, Louisa's first impression of a man was an appraiser's

impression, and as the years went by and she met fewer and fewer men this impression was invariably favorable. Yes, he would do. Not, of course, anything like her ideal, but the imagination was always, thank God, adaptable and could, after a little coaxing, make romance of very little. She did not want definitely a husband, indeed she was frightened at the idea, but she wanted something special in her life if it was only a blighted love, something to which poetry could cling. So now public opinion was forcing her to cling to Blaine Decker, obliging her to feel as hurt and wretched over his coolness as if she actually did love him. When he passed her absently in the school corridors the students winked to indicate this indifference was just a pose, but Louisa, torn between what she realized they were thinking and what she knew was true, scarcely knew how to act. Most of the time she resented Decker's failure to accept the role allotted to him and though he was undoubtedly a marvel of wit and brilliance, nevertheless it did seem a little stupid of him not to know what was being said about him and either play up to his reputation or be properly embarrassed about it.

In her bedroom at The Oaks, dressing with the other teachers for Laurie Neville's party, she blushed at the allusions to Decker.

"Will you go with us or is the boyfriend calling for you?" Miss Swasey wanted to know. She and Miss Emmons had spent the afternoon giving each other facials, manicures and shampoos, and having admired themselves in their own mirrors now completed examinations of their evening toilettes before Louisa's long mirror. Not that it made any difference how they looked, Miss Emmons observed, since whatever new men there were present would be delegated to Laurie herself or to Miss Manning. Miss Swasey looked complacently at her pretty throat in the mirror, trying her curly brown hair back over her ears, then pulling it forward again.

"I think we should look nice on account of the parents," she said gently. "After all a lot of trustees and board members

will be there and they notice if we don't look right. That's all I
care about."

Miss Emmons was silent, reminded that it had taken her
twelve years of teaching in Dell River to get over delusions such as
the younger teacher cherished. Now she was able to speak out
openly and with a bitter gaiety about "getting a man." She could
boast of the school janitor's compliments to her, she whispered of
farmers who stared at her legs when she got on the Cross-State
bus, she loudly proclaimed her devotion to the primitive types,
and what she would do if she ever had the money to go on a
Polynesian tour. This frankness more insistent and more unnat-
ural than her original shyness made Miss Murrell shudder. Louisa
thought, "I would rather never see a man than admit it mattered
so much to me; and to go screaming around that you like someone just because he's a man—instead of a—well, a *person*—is
frightful . . . The way she jokes about the football boys . . . How
awful if Professor Decker should hear her sometime."

If he should hear them asking about him as if he were her
property he'd never dare to even speak to her again, Louisa
thought, and if Mrs. Benjamin knew what everyone said—but
it occurred to Louisa that Mrs. Benjamin heard only what she
wished to hear, a marvelous device for converting all sensations
to pleasure. Sometimes, as now, vaguely hurt because Professor
Decker did not know she existed yet she must blush and lower
her eyes every time Emmons or Swasey mentioned him, sometimes Louisa wondered why she had agreed so unquestioningly
with Mrs. Benjamin's and Decker's estimates of themselves as
great figures. Certainly neither Swasey nor Emmons would be
trembling with pleasure at the prospect of a Sunday evening at
the Benjamins' simple home. Nor, Louisa reflected, pinning
down the neck of Laurie Neville's black crepe with her pearl
bar so as to make it more of an evening dress, would they feel as
she could not help feeling, that for Mrs. Benjamin to appear at
Laurie Neville's musical evening gave the affair a certain professional stamp.

Connie's own feeling was the same. She was glad to show Laurie that she approved of her gallant attempts to make Dell River a music center; it seemed to her there had been a touch of deference about the invitation, as if Miss Neville and her companion scarcely dared hope that their simple entertainment could interest a genuine artist. Connie wanted to assure them that she was not at all proud, that indeed she thought Miss Neville's interest in music a very encouraging sign in this section and in this age. She would show this opinion, of course, by her mere presence. She thought of seeing Decker there, of talking it over with him, and there in the crowded drawing room capturing their rhythm once again. She saw tonight as something upon which they would fasten next Sunday night—he and Louisa and she. So eager was she for next Sunday's discussion of tonight that the present seemed endless, she could endure it only by marking each detail for future description, the walk through the frosty blue night to the mansion seemed unending, the thought that this was only the beginning of the occasion was hardly to be borne. Helen took quick excited steps beside her—there had been no use inviting Gus to come, he was interested neither in Miss Neville or society. Helen wanted to go because the Marshall girls had gone there once with their parents and she had never been there; she thought there might be dancing and Laurie Neville's city friends would undoubtedly be there doing all the latest steps and she could learn just by watching and astound the girls in the Domestic Science kitchen tomorrow by demonstration.

They hurried up little side streets and where lights were shining in windows Helen would say, jealously, "They must be going, too! Why were *they* asked?" Next Sunday, Connie thought, she would tell Decker how exquisitely the crescent moon decorated the bare twisted branches of the huge oak on the hill; this tiny rim of silver caught, like an antique brooch, in the deep velvet of the winter sky, could not light the Dell River night, yet the houses and their hedges were outlined in a frosty

phosphorescent glow that came from the sky somehow, perhaps
from millions of invisible stars massed behind the curtain,
burning it through with their collected radiance. She pulled the
white chiffon scarf over her hair so that the occasional wandering snowflakes would not disarrange her and absently slipped
her hand through Helen's hard little arm.

"There!" said Helen and they were at the carriage entrance
of the old Neville mansion. For a moment Connie had a curious feeling of being in a play, of being that lost daughter who
returns on a winter night with her child to weep at the family
gates that once closed upon her. Already she reduced the feeling
to words for Decker, saw his appreciative amusement in
advance and then shivered, for it struck her for the first time
how much this huge iron gate revealing the gay lights from the
house with an involved lace pattern was like her grandfather's
iron gate. She thought if she were Laurie Neville with that
great estate she would tear down all gates for they did not keep
trespassers out, they only made the dwellers prisoners.

"Poor Laurie Neville!" she thought. "She never had a Tony
to free her from those gates."

They walked up the snow-sprinkled cinder path to the
square brick house. In the glare of a dozen automobile headlights, bereaved of its ivy vines, it looked bare and unfriendly;
any stranger would know that here was a house accustomed to
being boarded up, any passer-by would guess that the chill of
many funerals would cling to these walls, that in a stupendous
gilded what-not inside the door would be tiny jade and ivory
figurines, Rogers' groups and painted Italian fans brought
home by traveled ancestors, that upstairs visitors would be
amazed by an old parlor organ and would inevitably experiment
with "viola," "vox humana" and all the beautifully named stops
that seldom worked. A sad familiar house, Connie thought,
known all over the world with little variation in either
architecture or history. She wondered if somewhere in middle
Massachusetts there might not be a Decker family house like

this, but there had never been for the Deckers anything but a small decent home with its women complaining of it.

"This is like my old home, dear," Connie said.

Helen turned her skeptical, pretty little face away. "Sure," she said enigmatically.

She thought, in a little burst of rage, that she wouldn't mind Mama talking so affectedly all the time if she would only come out and be natural at least with her own daughter. She wouldn't care, Helen thought, if the whole Greene family had lived in a barn (very likely they had)—but why couldn't Mama come out and say as much? She, Helen, would have said so and if people didn't like it they could lump it. What bothered Helen was not where her ancestors lived but where she herself lived. The present was the important thing. And right now she hated her mother for being so complacent about where *she* had been brought up, when she made no attempt to give her own children the same luxury. She might have nagged Papa, at least, into being something besides a shoemaker—say he ran a dry goods store or something that would give his daughters free silk stockings. . . .

At the front door they rang the bell and waited. Helen felt her resentment diminishing in the noisy excitement released with the opening of the door, but even with her mother's fingers gently pressing her arm she would not relent completely, The idea whirred around in her head, "I could have lived in such a place as this instead of only visiting it. I would have had a chance if Mother hadn't been so hot after her own chances. And she's happy and satisfied instead of being ashamed of her selfishness!"

They went in together and Miss Manning, standing by the piano, commented to Laurie Neville and Louisa beside her, "Mrs. Benjamin and her daughter, Laurie. Don't look right now, but doesn't it seem sweet and old-fashioned to see mother and daughter coming in together, arm in arm, perfectly at ease with each other?"

"A perfect picture," agreed Laurie, glancing in their direction. Louisa Murrell blushed as if any compliment for her dear friend was a compliment for her, too.

⚬

They were safe at last, their old ground once more restored. Happily they shivered in the windowseat of the Neville drawing room, sipping their glasses of California wine, nibbling their lettuce sandwiches, chatting in rather high-pitched tones of matters they thought suitable to this occasion. Louisa Murrell fluttered near them and shut her ears to the others. Here in this little corner by the glass miniature case one could believe in civilization, she thought gratefully, just being near Mrs. Benjamin and Decker one could swear that most people were fine, sensitive souls, that in Dell River beauty could thrive as well as in great cities. If one looked around one saw Dell River, stiff, uncomfortable, harassed by the thought of listening to music, wistfully looking toward the card-room or openly suggesting a rubber of bridge to escape the tedium of a set program. There was Helen, reduced to wandering drearily about the house with Hank Herbert, a lanky chinless boy she had passionately hated for years but what could one do—he was the only other young person present . . . and he did have a dandy plan for skipping out to the back dining room with the portable victrola later on; he figured the musicians would drown out the sound of the victrola so no one could catch them in the other room dancing. . . .

"They're fair entertainers," Decker explained to Mrs. Benjamin. "Not bad musicians, really, but not first-rate by any means."

"Of course not!" agreed Mrs. Benjamin and they both laughed a little sadly thinking of days they could have revelled in first-rate performances. Decker offered her a cigarette and as always Connie hesitated, as if, inveterate smoker though she was, she would reject the temptation this once, so she gently shook her head.

"You look amazingly well tonight, my dear lady," observed Decker—eying her with the air of a connoisseur. She wore her old blue embroidered Spanish shawl over a black silk dress. "That shawl's a rather rare design, isn't it? I had a friend once—you've probably seen her picture in the paper a dozen times—Ilsa Darmster?"

"I know the name," said Connie politely.

"She had a similar shawl. She used to say, 'Blaine, there isn't another shawl like this in all Spain.' I must tell you about Ilsa sometime. A curious woman—but fascinating." Here Decker blew a ring of smoke in the air and gazed meditatively after it. "Ilsa was a very strange character indeed."

Louisa, leaning on the back of a chair, listened eagerly, rapidly throwing together in her fancy an Ilsa Darmster, like a stage carpenter building a set from a playwright's limited description. Tall, long-nosed, with dozens of gold bracelets, long antique earrings that clinked against a jewelled comb thrust in her sleek black hair—that was Louisa's Ilsa Darmster—a drawling voice punctuated with a low, rather sinister laugh, a green velvet, excessively low-cut dress, and a volume of Baudelaire in her long, coral-tipped fingers. Ilsa Darmster. Oh, thank you, thank you, Blaine Decker.

Louisa sighed under her breath, for this new invention, this lovely new person to find in Dell River. The four musicians began to play and dreamily Louisa leaned on the chair, thinking of the new, fascinating friend Decker had given her.

Decker whispered to the two ladies that Laurie had heard the quartet in a Lyceum program near Pittsburgh and thought, since they were touring nearby, it would be a good chance to bring them to Dell River. Decker lounged back against the window, smoking with half-closed eyes, listening, Louisa thought admiringly, with his whole body. Mrs. Benjamin's chin was in her cupped hand, she gazed so intently at the musicians

that the dark violinist muttered something to the 'cellist, but
Connie did not see or hear, she was thinking of Ilsa Darmster
and for her Ilsa was built majestically, a Brunhilda with glorious golden hair and blue eyes, she walked up and down the
deck of the ocean liner with a man's coat and hair streaming,
she looked like a Viking princess and when she spoke there was
a husky, vibrant quality in her voice that made everyone know
she was a singer, or perhaps an actress. Ilsa . . . A wave of gratitude to Decker for the lovely dolls he gave her swept over
Connie. She smiled absently at the violinist and saw the sea
beyond him, blue tumbling waves that crashed into the fairy
music of a Chinese wind bell—but no, that was the violin. She
caught Louisa's eye and they smiled vaguely at each other, their
Ilsa Darmsters met somewhere on a Mozart phrase and bowed,
dissolved once more into music.

"Not bad at all, you know," Decker commented to the
ladies, applauding with the rest of the guests, most of whom felt
that bad or good, it was all exceedingly dull and with a big
room like this and musicians a dance would have been so much
nicer. He looked for approbation toward Mrs. Benjamin.
Connie inclined her head thoughtfully to indicate that after
proper deliberation she might approve this program but would
not rush into a hasty condemnation or approval. Miss Manning,
in a severely cut black velvet, unobtrusively filled Decker's glass
once more and moved away. Decker moved the glass about
under his nose and closed his eyes appreciatively.

"Excellent wine," he whispered to Connie. "I'll venture it's
as good as the average table wine in the best foreign restaurants.
Miss Neville is a marvel, the way, quietly here in Dell River, she
maintains a perfectly cosmopolitan standard. Take this wine—I
must ask her if it isn't left over from her pre-war stock. I'm positive it's at least ten years old."

Mr. Decker illustrated his point by finishing the glass deftly,
in a silent toast to Miss Neville who was passing. Laurie wandered among the guests, fully aware of their discomfort, trying

to speak to groups knotted here and there, but conscious of the chill she spread she caught Gertrude Manning's arm and whispered desperately, "Why do they always stop talking when I come up? They make me feel like Teacher spying on them while they cheat. . . . Why must people treat me this way as if I were a plague! I'll never have another party—never."

"A lovely party, Laurie," Miss Manning said, firmly grasping the other's elbow. "I was just thinking we must entertain more so that the town people get to know you better."

"Always I must make these mistakes," Laurie rushed on in a little sobbing whisper while her companion smiled fixedly to show that they were merely having a friendly chat. "I open up to people and they hate me. I tell you they all hate me. Dell River will never take me in—look how stiff they are—just look—"

The musicians were playing some Italian songs and the violinist put down his fiddle and sang. Connie listened with a rapt face.

"'Come back to Sorrento,'" she whispered to Decker. "You know that's the song Manuel used to sing. Imagine hearing it after all these years."

Judicially they discussed the man's voice, decided he was rather good, though Decker deferred to Connie on this point. They did agree that it was possible to find as many good things in this little village as anywhere in the world.

Decker saw Marshall and his stout wife approaching and waved his hand patronizingly.

"Marshall's not a bad sort, you know," he confided in Miss Murrell who prayed for the day to come when she would no longer be terrified of the school principal. "A man without background, of course, but not bad for here, not bad at all. Impossible socially but that's only the fault of his training."

He was sorry now that Miss Manning had decided not to sing for he felt like showing Marshall how much more at home he, Decker, was in a salon than the principal himself. He was radiantly happy with Connie and the reverent Louisa hanging upon his every word. He could face any situation with these two ladies' perpetual testimony that Blaine Decker was a most extraordinary man.

He observed Mrs. Benjamin going up to the singer as they picked up their instruments to close the program. He heard her grave compliments to the singer, the carefully considered praise of one great artist to another. The musicians beamed but the violinist's eye roved speculatively over Connie's rich, graceful figure. Connie saw that they were not as impressed with her approval as they might be so she added, with a smile, "You see I know good things for I'm a musician myself. I sang for Morini—in fact I once sang the song you gave this evening—'Come back to Sorrento'—I've forgotten the words now but —"

The 'cellist, a pallid gray blonde, pressed eagerly toward her. "You say you were a concert singer?"

Connie hesitated.

"Not exactly," she admitted finally, smiling reassuringly as if she had dismissed that particular role as inferior. "Hardly that."

"I didn't catch your name," the 'cellist insisted, for so often in just such little places as this one discovered fallen stars. Again Connie hesitated and twisted the fringe of the blue Spanish shawl. "Benjamin—Madame Benjamin," she said softly.

She saw Decker and Miss Murrell wandering restlessly toward the door so she broke away, leaving the men with hands to their foreheads trying to place the name "Madame Benjamin" in concert history. The violinist gave it up with a shrug and looked after Madame Benjamin's departing form.

"Not bad," he muttered to his companion. It was his theory that there was a practical base to feminine musical appreciation.

Connie saw herself in a long gilt hall mirror and now that Decker had admired the shawl she saw herself as a very distinguished-looking woman; these musicians had unquestionably recognized her as someone of importance and she was glad she had been able to congratulate them in perfect sincerity, for who knew better than herself the necessity to the artist of intelligent appreciation? She recalled the 'cellist's face as she had told him her name—Madame Benjamin; it was difficult to believe that he would not eventually place her as a famous Isolde of former years. She stood beside Decker and Miss Murrell in the chilly hallway. Decker leaned against the stair newel-post, his arm negligently around it, the other clasping his wine glass. He was flushed and perfectly content for he was telling Miss Murrell of the first time he had heard Paderewski, of fabulous musicales he had attended in Paris and Leipzig in the company of Starr Donnell, the novelist, and Ilsa Darmster, who never wore stockings; he referred in passing to the satires of Mozart, the unfinished opera of Rimsky-Korsakoff, and then, finishing off his glass of wine with a fine gesture, he listed out of sheer splendid extravagance a dozen composers, giving them their full names and hyphens.

Louisa was dazzled and so happy that she was afraid Miss Swasey or Miss Emmons might see the tears in her eyes from across the room. Her ears hummed with Decker's voice, her lonely mind eagerly collected his jeweled allusions, decorated itself with the names of Russian composers, arranged a permanent altar for Ilsa Darmster, the goddess of glamor. Thank you, oh, thank you again, dear Decker, she thought, for Mozart and Rimsky-Korsakoff, for St. Julienne and Lachrymae Cristi, for all the beautiful names to shine in dark minds.

Connie Benjamin kept nodding in sympathetic understanding. The musicians had gone to their train and guests were gladly going home. Laurie Neville kept a tight hold of Gertrude Manning's arm and did not scream as she so much wanted to, because no matter what she did, no matter how she tried, Dell River would not have her, she must always be its freak, someone to be pointed at, exploited, or at best soothed as if she was a sanitarium case, well she was, she was, she WAS, and she was going to scream—scream—but she couldn't scream after Gertrude had decided to sing and that was what was happening.

Professor Decker, very red and very strange-looking, sat on the piano bench and varied his accompaniments with a spontaneous vibrato in the treble chords and occasionally was moved to impromptu trills while Miss Manning bravely held a high note to which she was not accustomed. "Jeune fillette—profitez du temps," she sang. She did not really think she could sing but she could read music and music of any sort kept Laurie Neville's hysteria in check. Laurie had joined Mrs. Benjamin and Louisa on the staircase. Louisa said that she had never realized how well Professor Decker played and Mrs. Benjamin agreed, adding that she herself had studied music years ago, that she had been at one time on the verge of a great career.

"I sang in English and a little Italian—my teacher was an Italian," she whispered confidentially. "For instance that song tonight—'Sorrento'—that was an old favorite of mine."

"Amazing!" replied Miss Neville, and then Decker and Miss Manning left the piano since the latter was deeply concerned about Laurie's desperately white face. Decker helped himself to another glass of wine at the buffet-table and then glanced up to meet the sad understanding look in Connie's eye, her tired amused smile—"My dear, think of it—you with your genius, here playing for a handful of stupid provincials who refuse to even listen, when actually you belong in Carnegie Hall! My poor precious Decker—lost here—completely lost!" Her smile said all this and more.

Helen had vanished long ago. Vaguely Connie remembered seeing her hurry out the door with a tall boy some time ago. She must follow her home, so Miss Manning went with her to the big damp upstairs bedroom where the coats had been piled on a great walnut four-poster bed. In a cracked gilded mirror Connie adjusted the white chiffon scarf about her face—a sweet face, Miss Manning thought, a sweet gentle face like a child's.

Decker waited downstairs and it was after they had said goodnight that he remembered his coat.

"Let me get it," Miss Manning begged. "What was it like?"

Decker described his raincoat, described in particular the London label although his coat could more easily have been identified by its shabbiness. Miss Manning could not find such a coat anywhere. She sent others in quest of it, even Mr. Herbert, the candy store man, who was slightly intoxicated and intended to stay till he was more so. But no London coat could be found.

"It seems a little odd," said Decker in restrained indignation, "that any of Miss Neville's guests would take a coat. After all it's rather hard to replace a London ulster, you know."

"It is indeed," said Miss Manning, and searched again, while Laurie went upstairs for a double bromide—in a little while she might burst into tears but at least that was more discreet than screaming. . . . The coat was not to be found. The only one left was a brown one with a belted back and a patch under one sleeve. A sickening wave of recognition came over Decker.

"Does it have a London label?" he asked weakly.

No. Instead of a London label, Miss Manning laughed, there was the mark of the People's Big Store in Lima. Moreover a man's name was sewn on the collar—"George Almon."

"Not mine," Decker said. "Oh, dear no."

Everyone was looking at him and after he had been so fussy about that London trademark he could not claim this one.

"But it doesn't matter —" he said with a wan smile.

So Mrs. Marshall's brother's coat was left indefinitely at the Neville house, thrown over the gardener's head on a stormy day, used as a cozy bed by the dogs, worn by Mrs. Busch when she hung up the clothes and all in all made a familiar note in the Neville back hall. Decker, a little drunk, pulled up his jacket collar and walked with Connie Benjamin on the left and Louisa on the right through the still cold midnight. The light dry snow crackled under their feet while Decker, with chattering teeth,

told them of the time Ilsa Darmster astounded Vienna or
Munich or possibly Berlin by dancing her New World dance
right out in the snow, clad only in one brilliant green veil.

↝

The second notice in the *Billboard* read:

> "Tony: Please let me hear from you through this
> paper. Still have your scarf after all these years.
> Constance."

Connie had sent this paragraph because the violinist had
reminded her of Tony, and the notion had somehow taken
hold of her that Tony was near her, else why did she think of
him so persistently? She began adjusting her memories to fit in
with Decker's theories that she had been madly in love with
Tony. A career lost because of a great love, she thought, and
wondered if after all it hadn't been worth it. As a photogra-
pher erases unflattering lines and defects in a portrait so
Connie revised her recollections of Tony, changed the brutality
of his desertion into a sensitive boy's anguish over being unable
to support a wife. She had never been resentful of his actions
any more than she had felt bitter toward her grandfather—
these defeats had crushed her so completely that they lost all
personal quality and became part of the relentless routine of a
grim destiny. She remembered well the fatigue in her ankles
and in the balls of her feet after walking blindly up and down,
anesthetizing her mind with the rhythmic clock-clock of her
high heels on the Board Walk, she remembered the blank ache
in her head, the curious weight on her chest that made her
bend her head as if it were a real burden. But the actual shocks
were forgotten.

She remembered the day she reached Marblehead when the
ocean wind became too much for her and her legs quietly

folded up. She was neither grateful nor surprised when the round-faced little foreigner—German or Jewish, she was uncertain which—helped her across a frosty field into someone's house. She did not care when he explained to the woman, "My wife just fainted," though later on she marveled that such a stolid man as Gus should be so discreetly efficient, taken it for granted that she was sick and in trouble, ready to accept any direction, kind or cruel. In her life all events seemed final and prearranged. It was arranged that some man should save her, marry her, and so, it developed, bring her to Dell River to peace, a peace in which past years were drowned, sensations past and present lost. After that first baby miscarried, Tony himself was erased, he was only a name until Decker had decorated him with the glamorous garlands of first love. So she had not only missed by a mere hair's breadth, great fame—she had also known a great love. Tony. Without Decker she would never have realized this.

The violinist at Laurie Neville's party had reminded her of Tony. His image replaced Tony's vaguely in her mind and both were lost when a poster went up in the Music Store carrying a picture of one Tyler Stewart, whose "Colonial Days" entertainers were coming to play in the school auditorium. The school children were urged to attend these two performances partly for their cultural value (some singing, a one-act operetta, a "reading" or two) and also because half the proceeds went to the school board in lieu of a fixed rental.

Decker spoke of this affair at Connie's on Sunday night.

"I understand this fellow Stewart sings fairly well," he informed her. "Old English things and all that. It might be well for you to drop in. I'd seriously like to know what your opinion is. Of course I've heard him rehearsing but—well, I'd like a really professional opinion of his work."

Mimi and Helen went to the matinee but Helen would not let Mimi sit with her after they arrived because none of her crowd wanted younger sisters tagging along so Mimi sat alone, reasonably content, and Helen with the older students crowded in the front rows, laughed, waved to friends in the balcony, popped paper bags, stamped their feet rhythmically till the curtain rose and all in all enjoyed to the full the jolly privileges of age.

Connie arrived only for the songs, as Decker had recommended. She wore the little worn sealskin capelet that she'd worn as a girl, and a little turban to match, its bald spots disguised by a dotted veil. She slipped in the dark hall and sat by herself in the back though even in the shadow she recognized Decker's figure standing in the back of the house, his arms folded. Mr. Marshall, present in his capacity of official manager of the auditorium but always slightly alarmed when it took on the gay aspect of a theatre, saw Mrs. Benjamin enter and was so impressed by her late arrival and the suggestion of quiet importance in her bearing that he hurried to where she sat and whispered apologetically to her, his program discreetly held up to his face, "It's really a very good little company, Mrs. Benjamin—no one could possibly take offense—and very instructive—many schools and women's clubs have had them purely for educational reasons. They tell me Tyler Stewart is a great favorite in the West, where he used to play in light opera. I think you'll be interested in his songs—of course he's no Caruso but I heard him rehearsing this morning and actually you could hear him all the way down to the Candy Store. I was astonished!"

"Really!" said Connie, and then the artist made his appearance in Colonial costume and Marshall tiptoed hastily back to his seat and found himself watching Mrs. Benjamin anxiously across the hall to see how she took the performance. Afterwards he wondered why this lady's reactions seemed so important, after all she was not a board member or a Miss Neville . . . it must be the way she came into the hall, her dignified air of authority and then there was all that talk of her being musical.

Connie felt that aside from the school children who naturally would not know, the audience was as conscious of her
presence as Mr. Marshall was, and the subdued gratification
this gave her made her only dimly alive to Tyler Stewart. In his
white wig and red sateen coat he looked darkly beautiful, far
more handsome than his poster in the Music Store, and Connie
thought if it had been this man instead of Tony who carried her
away everything would have been different, their ambitions
would have united them and made them both stronger, they
might have been concert singers together. But no sooner had
she conjured this picture than she was tired of the weight of
success and lonely for Helen and for Mimi whom she saw now
watching the stage with a resigned bored little face; she thought
it was nicer to be listening with Decker to someone else sing
than to be the solitary performer.

"My love is like a red, red rose," sang Tyler Stewart, holding his palms together as in prayer and swaying from side to
side, "that newly blooms in June. My love is like a mel-o-dy—"

Tears came to Connie's eyes and she bent quickly over the
program for she did not want the watching Mr. Marshall to suspect that the song reminded her of the great love that had been in
her life, she wanted him to believe that her attitude toward music
was more gravely critical. She did not mind so much that Decker
should guess her emotion, for it was Decker who had made of
her early mistake a great love, and she knew intuitively that no
matter how angry her feeling might make him it was really what
he wanted to see, the very thing he expected of women with
great loves in their past. . . . She would put a third notice in that
magazine for Tony, she decided, but when he did come back to
her she would never dare let Decker know she had summoned
him, he must believe it was Tony who had done the seeking. Still,
the other way revealed how weak she was in a romantic, feminine way and she knew this angered and flattered him curiously.
. . . She did not applaud the song for she would not decide till the
end whether this singer was really worthy of her praise.

Mr. Stewart sang operatic airs, he sang *La Donna è Mobile* and Connie allowed herself to bend forward on this, intently critical, he sang old English songs and many a spirited ballad with a chorus of staccato "la-la-la-la-la-la's," while the profiles of Mr. Marshall and Decker were turned in Mrs. Benjamin's direction to see if the way she now leaned back in her seat indicated disapproval. In the interval of applause while a smiling girl in a pink shepherdess costume played "The Rustle of Spring" Mr. Marshall hurried over to Mrs. Benjamin again and Decker, twisting his moustache, followed.

"What's the verdict, Mrs. Benjamin?" whispered Mr. Marshall anxiously. "He is really excellent, don't you think? After all we have so little music here, you know, that we ought to be grateful for a gifted fellow like Stewart. He does very well, don't you think?" Connie nodded her head judicially.

"Quite well," she answered with a kind smile. "It's hard to judge a man's voice unless you've heard him in other things, as well."

"A different type of program," agreed Decker. "I think as Mrs. Benjamin does, Marshall. The man is fair but the upper tones—"

"The upper register, exactly!" Connie said. "Still he does have feeling . . . a great deal of feeling. And that counts for so much."

She sighed thinking that it was so true that love was like a melody.

"It makes up for everything," stoutly asserted Marshall, looking savagely at Decker. "And wait till you hear his next group. I tell you we're very fortunate in getting him."

He was ruffled and his spirits a little dashed by Mrs. Benjamin's quiet little answering smile. He might not know music but he was the one who ran the hall, he heard the rehearsals of everything that came to town and if it weren't for him these superior people like Decker and Mrs. Benjamin wouldn't hear anything at all, he'd like to tell them that, too. . . .

He resumed his seat and was aware of Decker standing behind him with folded arms in that irritating Napoleonic pose of his.

"On the road to Mandalay—" sang Mr. Stewart after the scene from *Eugenie Grandet* had been acted out thoroughly by the company, "where the flying fishes play—" whereupon the highschool boys stamped their feet, whistled and shouted their applause. Marshall twisted his head and motioned Decker to lean forward while he whispered "Might be a good thing to have in the Boys' Chorus for Easter Exercises."

Decker smiled dubiously—he hated the implication that he needed any outside suggestions in his own department.

"Hmmm . . . Possibly. Quite possibly," he answered and Marshall ground his teeth at the arrogance of his tone, as if what was good enough for a fellow like Tyler Stewart might not be up to Professor Decker's musical standard. Conscious of having impressed the principal, Decker drew back and leaned against a pillar while the artist with imploring eyes and a slight sob in his voice sang, as encore, an old love song so tenderly that Connie shut her eyes to guard the to tears and pictures of Tony flickered on the insides of her eyelids, though, to tell the truth Tony had never spoken of love, being inarticulate about all his emotions but anger. At the end of the performance Connie knew that Decker was waiting to walk home with her but she could not resist an impulse that had occurred to her when the curtain dropped. Before the lights were on she hurried quietly out and around the building to a back door leading to a school storeroom used as dressing room for the stage performances. She had stumbled into the cast dressing room where the three ladies and two men (sensibilities assuaged by a battered burlap screen used for segregational purposes) were throwing white wigs and tarnished metal cloth costumes into a great open trunk. There was no sign of Stewart.

"He's in the furnace room—the star's room," said one man, looking rather curiously at Connie. "Does he know you're coming?"

"No," said Connie. "Will you be good enough to tell him—
ah—Madame Benjamin would like to congratulate him?"

She was getting used to the sound of Madame now and
regretted not having thought to use it years ago since there was
no harm in it and it did give one a sense of dignity impossible to
find in a simple "Mrs." She saw the actor look curiously at her
and then he went down two steps to knock at the furnace-room
door, planting his knuckles firmly on the black chalked letters
"KEEP OUT." He stuck his head inside then motioned Connie
to go on in.

Gravely Connie entered the furnace-room and saw Tyler
Stewart in a black velvet dressing-gown, that had unquestionably seen many and better days, standing in a corner where the
twilight filtering through the basement window could mistily
enhance his failing beauty. The gray furnace sending huge gray
arms across the ceiling gave her a slight chill, it was like a giant
octopus and in the dim light augmented by one small blue elec-
tric bulb Tyler Stewart seemed more sinister than beautiful.
She saw that he was older than he appeared on the stage and his
hair was dyed so black and curled so rigidly, even his black roving eyes must have been touched up with some unknown
chemical. His costume hung on a hanger attached to a water
pipe and the vivid blue suit he was about to wear hung on
another pipe. A small mirror was propped up on a ledge by the
narrow barred window and a tin of cold cream was beside it.
He was lighting a cigarette as Connie came in, and looked at
her obliquely over the flaming match.

"Madame Benjamin?"

Connie inclined her head. Now she felt completely at ease,
the gracious patron of the arts.

"I came to tell you how much I appreciated your work, Mr.
Stewart. We hear so little first rate talent, you know, here—it
was a perfect performance."

Mr. Stewart disclaimed perfection with a wave of the hand
and a modest smile.

"You see," pursued Connie with a sigh, "when one has been so close to professional singing as I have—ah yes, I sang for Morini at one time—'The throat of an artist' was what he said. But it was not to be. . . . However, you can understand that I have the professional point of view and know a real singer when I hear one."

"Thank you," said Stewart and studied his visitor with frank curiosity.

"You still sing?" he inquired.

Connie lifted a shoulder with a deprecatory smile.

"I keep in touch with things, of course," she said. "I might go back into it again though I'm afraid I'm needed far too much at home."

"You do give occasional concerts then?"

Connie frowned.

"Not exactly," she said and added quickly, "I act as sort of musical advisor to my friends—I'm by no means out of the music field just because I live in this odd little place. One can keep up, you know."

"I see."

Connie was vaguely disturbed by his unresponsiveness, and by his roving eye which seemed to be waiting for some cue, as if what she was saying was not convincing and he expected the real cause of her visit to be revealed any minute. She tried to say something, something to sustain her original feeling of assuranceand polite superiority but Stewart's expectant attitude was not helping her. Someone knocked on the door and Stewart hurried over and spoke to someone outside in a low tone. The door closed again and then Connie said as he came back to her, "I sang 'My love is like a red rose' at one time myself, but I really enjoy the arias more, don't you, Mr, Stewart? If I had kept up with my career nothing would have satisfied me but opera."

"Is that a fact?" said Stewart and poured himself a drink of water from a china pitcher on the stool. He drank it leaning

back against the gray stone basement walls, his eyes on Connie
with a quick calculating look that made her feel curiously
defensive. She said, "I hope you will forgive my intruding but I
wanted you to know how much your singing meant to me. I—
I thank you for it."

Tyler bowed stiffly and murmured something she did not
understand.

There was nothing more to be said so he stood waiting
either for her to continue or to leave. Dissatisfied and embarrassed Connie turned to leave. Stewart followed her to the door,
smoking his cigarette. He took the hand she extended in
farewell and held it a moment.

"When do you want to come again?" His voice was so low
and silky that the meaning did not penetrate her mind at first.
"I think we understand each other, don't we?"

Connie put her hands out frantically against him but he
caught them and kissed her mouth lingeringly, smiling a little
because he knew so well the favor he was bestowing and
because women were so transparent. . . . Someone turned the
knob of the door and Connie stumbled out as the actor entered.
She remembered to smile brightly at the players dressing in the
gymnasium and not to reveal by the horror in her eyes the quite
dreadful thing that had happened to her. When she came out
on the street it was dark and she ran down the nearest byway
crying out softly "Oh . . . oh . . . oh," then remembered to put
her hand over her mouth so that no one could hear. In the
unexpected glow of a street corner lamp she recognized
Decker leaning against the post waiting for her. She couldn't see
him now, she couldn't possibly talk to him lest he should suspect that Madame Benjamin, the artist, had been so hideously
mistaken for Mrs. Benjamin, the woman. She turned quickly
up an alley and ran.

In the shadow of Mrs. Busch's house she saw a man
embracing a girl. Her heart pounding and her whole body
aching as if bruised merely by a sensual look, she reached her

own door, the refuge of her own living room. She pulled the gloves from her trembling fingers and sat down to the piano. Desperately she began to play in the darkness, singing in a choked and shaking voice—"La donna è mobile-la-la-lala—"

✧

Connie was ill. Gus wanted to call in the doctor but she would not hear of it for she did not know how to describe her symptoms. Was it a disease to be afraid to face people, was there a prescription for terror, for shame so intense, so fatiguing that she could not stand on her two legs? The third day in bed she received a note and roses from The Oaks' own hothouse from Louisa Murrell but no word came from Decker. Connie knew he must have seen her go into Tyler Stewart's dressing room and evade him afterward, and no matter what he may have thought of this she was grateful to him for staying away. She could not have faced him and confessed—"I went to him to discuss music and he thought I only came to be kissed."

Shame poured through her body when she recalled Stewart's eyes as she talked of songs. How could she have mistaken that look for deference? She could scarcely face Gus who sat patiently at the foot of her bed every night while she tried to drink the hot milk Mimi prepared.

"No cough, no headache—just a little fever—I don't understand this," Gus shook his head in great perplexity. "If you can't get up tomorrow I'm going to send in the doctor no matter what you say."

Connie patted his hand reassuringly. She could not explain that this weakness must persist until her mind came upon some philosophy that would banish shame. In the darkness it grew worse, for Stewart's avid eyes became the violinist's eyes, then Tony's eyes, then changed into Blaine Decker's eyes, none of them looking up to her admiringly as an artist but hungrily as if she were any woman.

"Only Gus," she thought sadly. "In all the world Gus is the only one who knows what I might have been. To the rest I'm like any other woman—Mrs. Busch—or Louisa."

Her veins burned, her eyes were hot aching stones from unshed tears, it seemed to her for the first time she was conscious of her body, a body that was Connie Benjamin in some curious way almost as music was Connie Benjamin. The consciousness grew out of the remembered look in men's eyes translated into meaning now for the first time. But it was not in Decker's eyes, strive as she might to collect the entire damning evidence she could not fairly credit him with desire. Yes, there was a difference in his admiration, he did see the Madame Benjamin, she gratefully admitted, and strength seemed to flow back into her with this quiet revelation. He did not think of her as accessible or desirable but as the artist—dear, dear Decker. . . . .

She lay facing the window watching the clouds blow over the moon, they played with different arrangements of gossamer as so many costumes for a spoiled prima donna. Connie dozed and when she opened her eyes a chilly shell pink stained the pale eastern sky. The dried brown rambler vines rattled against the window in the frigid dawn winds. Shell pink merged into amethyst and lemon and presently these shy colors shivered into a winter sun. Connie thought, "I am well—I can get up." Because of Decker, because he saw her as she wanted to be seen.

To Decker she was without gender, she thought contentedly. But why did he find her undesirable? Were there other women—say Laurie Neville or Ilsa Darmster whom he considered beautiful, women a man could love rather than revere? Connie could not remember her own face or form as she had never looked in the mirror for anything but the impression of dignity she wished to give. What did she really look like? What had Tyler Stewart seen—and the violinist and Tony—what had they found that was not enough for Blaine Decker?

Still a little uncertain of her legs Connie groped her way to the dresser and tipped the mirror so that she could see herself. What was it Stewart saw? The pallid daylight made a gray shadow of the mirror and she saw only dimly but it seemed to her that this was the first time she'd ever looked upon herself. She peered closer at her face and thought, "Why, I am beautiful." So this was Connie Benjamin, the woman. All these years she might have been happy in merely being beautiful, but she had never known. She tipped the mirror further back to see the outline of her body—richly curved yet slim. Her face in this light had the pearly translucence of a ghost, her dark hair tousled and uncombed looked wildly strange, her full mouth curiously brilliant. A ray of sunlight suddenly annihilated the misty perfection of this picture and with a contraction of pain in her heart she saw that the verbs describing her beauty must be in the past tense for there were lines near her eyes, the droop of lost youth in her mouth, in the contours of her cheek, her throat that a moment before seemed so indestructibly firm was circled with fine threads. She was overwhelmed with sadness to think these remaining charms were passing, and that all these years she must have been lovely without knowing it. She was old. Thirty-seven was old. In five more years more lines—in ten years what Tyler Stewart or violinist would look at her without disturbing appraisal . . . was it possible that any man, however crude, would glance at her ankles as she talked of music? And at forty-seven . . . Connie ran a finger slowly over her cheek. Even now the doom of age was upon her. She was saying farewell to a woman she'd never known, a woman, once beautiful, her beauty congealing into years until presently a man could only pity her as a Hellenic fragment no longer able to provoke tumult, admired only for its vanished loveliness. . . . The sun crept through the gnarled branches of the vine and cruelly found more signs of ruin, each reluctant ray brought a chill to the woman at the mirror, pointing out relentlessly the faults of age. So she had been a woman, a desirable woman . . .

and now that was over and the chill of approaching winter was to slowly creep over her as hemlock night steal slowly through her veins, the victim conscious of her fate, yet even up to the moment the hemlock reaches her heart she knows and suffers, she still can weep for her forlorn doom.

Now shame was lost in fear that this degradation would never happen again. And Decker who saw only the artist, who did not know her throat was white or her bosom charming . . . was he not stealing youth from her? And Gus who had never told her she was alluring. . . . After all had not Tyler Stewart done something kind for her in revealing her own vanishing treasures to herself? She had a feverish wish for day to come that she might send for Decker and watch him, just to see if she might not surprise that look in his eyes too before the sun betrayed her with further evidence of lost years.

⌁

Here was something again that could not be told to Decker. It puzzled Connie that no matter how swiftly they cleared the way of all secrets between them new reserves formed automatically, there could never be complete understanding between two persons, new barriers were built as fast as the old were torn down. She could not tell him of this change in her, this bewildering consciousness of her body, she could not explain the sensation of guilt she experienced whenever Gus referred now to his tenant.

When they met for the first time after Stewart's performance there was a certain restraint between them. Decker called on his way to a Saturday night buffet at Laurie Neville's. He could not explain to himself why he had not called during her illness but somehow he could not bear to see her disarmed. He had no interest in a sick woman, demanding of pity, her very weakness a disillusioning proof that she was only human and not the rare immortal he fancied. He felt bewildered and a little ashamed that for an invalided Mrs. Benjamin he had no tenderness but rather impatience that the dear routine of their companionship should be interrupted, indeed his own life thrown quite out of key for the moment. He could not imagine sitting beside her couch discussing physical disabilities with her, it would be impossible to assume more than a polite pretense of concern over her pains. The Mrs. Benjamin he reverenced was their joint invention and not subject to the infirmities of God-made beings.

"Perhaps I have no real sympathy for anyone," Decker mused and was rather proud of being above such sentimental limitations until he thought of a week years ago when Starr Donnell was in the hospital and he, Decker, sat at the foot of the bed, the heart torn out of his body with anguish, listening to Starr's tortured delirium. Yes, then he had believed in human afflictions and suffered for someone else.

So now he waited for the return of his Mrs. Benjamin, impatiently marking time for her vacation from Olympus. When he called he felt a wave of pleasure at seeing her almost as before, so well that there was no necessity for referring to her sickness. Indeed she wore convalescence as a lady should—a touch of spirituality in her pallor, a certain fragile delicacy combined with poise so that, Decker thought with relief, one was pleasantly conscious of one's masculine strength and, better yet, assured that no demands would be put upon it.

"I wanted to talk over Tyler Stewart's songs with you," he said, sitting on the arm of a chair, unwilling to allow himself the permanent commitment of a comfortable seat. "There were so many things that were good, for instance, his lyric quality—I looked for you afterward."

"Yes," said Connie and looked steadily at the jar of Jerusalem cherries Mimi had placed on the library table.

"Someone said you had gone back to speak to Stewart but I knew they were mistaken," Decker went on. He lit a cigarette and smiled at her—after all it was rather charming and in a way flattering for her to succumb to the usual feminine vapors, and the brief separation made him realize how comforting, how actually necessary this relationship was to him.

Connie returned the smile queerly, holding tight to the arms of her chair.

"Yes—I did go back to see him," she said in a strained voice. "I wanted to compliment him, of course. . . . You know how important that is. People here never think to tell the artist what he's meant to them. . . ."

It was nothing but she looked at him with such odd, frightened eyes, her face turned questioningly toward him as if waiting for a verdict, and Decker's heart seemed to stop, he swallowed two or three times but no words would come, and a shocking sensation of hatred for her overwhelmed him. He saw the feeling come up as one might see the approach of a huge steam roller, powerless before it, knowing this must be the end. Little doors opened, one, two, three, all along his brain . . . something had happened at that interview to upset her, that woman hurrying up the alley in the darkness that night had actually been Connie just as he first thought and she was running from him for some reason . . . lastly there was no escape from the rack of jealous, stabbing, frightful humiliating pain that she should have had some intimate experience, how-ever innocent, with that man, particularly someone so nearly glamorous. He saw it all coming, the jealousy, hate, love, like a dreaded but inescapable sickness, and afterwards this premo-nition was vaguely connected with a green flowerpot of Jerusalem cherries on a lace table-runner . . . his eyes fastened desperately to each external detail as if to distract him from inner revelations . . . he studied the scars and rings on the wal-nut veneer of the table, took in the red and fudgy-brown of a magazine cover and then stopped at the old unpainted door leading to the upstairs. It was when his eyes reached this door that the entire sensation struck him irrevocably—no protec-tion from jealousy or suspicion, no longer any armor against feeling. He could almost have wept at this defeat. Instead he said, "Isn't that strange, I've never noticed that the stair door is crooked. See? The whole door is at least three inches off the line."

"I never knew that," said Connie and they both studied the door intently. Then Decker remembered seven o'clock supper at Miss Neville's. For the first time Connie did not urge his staying or dropping in later in the evening. She examined the hall door as if nothing had ever been so vital as its dimensions. Decker got quickly to his feet, trying not to look at her or show his mounting indignation at the unexpected betrayal of their friendship.

"I felt that Stewart had a very slender talent," he said, and was angry to find he was stammering a little, "a very slender talent, indeed. I'm surprised you thought him important enough to visit. A very poor voice and a very poor program indeed."

"Yes, I know," said Connie simply and her face looked so pale and her mouth so weak that it was hard not to strike her, Decker thought. It was all very well for women to be fragile but to be deliberately so pliable and at the mercy of any stronger will was not decent. There was nothing one could do about such a woman, as quickly as one built her up she collapsed into a jelly—worse, far worse, than being definitely wanton, Decker reflected, at least there was something hard and dependable in a wanton. Then, too, one could hurt and be revenged upon a wanton but there was nothing to be done about a delicate, changing shadow.

"I suppose this man Stewart reminded you of your first romance," Decker said, fixing a smile on his face to indicate how amused he was by her poor little romances. "The same cheap theatrical type, doubtless. Once a taste is formed in women they invariably run true to form."

He saw that Connie's head drooped a little, evidently there was one way he could return wound for wound, but he knew there was for him not enough satisfaction in these feeble blows. Physical violence would be inadequate as well, and as for this shaming of her, there was a guilty confidence in her eyes, once fleetingly meeting his, that made a virtue of shame.

He left the house confused and angry. Now he saw his life fretted with desire and warped with jealousy, he saw the delicate threads of their friendship tangled with the new consciousness and now, leaving Connie, he could not sustain the warm, flattered knowledge that he had been brilliantly extraordinary, instead he carried a brutally distinct image of the blue of her gown against her disturbing white throat.

Abruptly Decker turned from the Neville gate and went back down the street to his own rooms. The corner was dark as it always was on Saturday night and he fumbled for the keyhole in the dim starlight. He stumbled up the staircase and turned on his living room light. The one light with its bluish shade made the room incredibly dreary and lonely. Decker dropped his hat on the table and leaned against the piano, his hand rumpled his hair in a vague, bewildered gesture. Something vital was slipping away, if he concentrated now he might win it back, he must regain it, for God knows there was little enough he could lose now. In the queer blue light his eyes found the portrait of his mother. There, that was one thing, though his heart rejected even this as being completely his. And Starr. With a twist of fear in his breast Decker thought, "In this room I have nothing, not even Starr. Starr never was. Paris never was. There was never anything but this village hidden far off alone and Mrs. Benjamin. She made the other things for me—she gave me myself with a past . . . but there was never anything but this present. . . . The Pilgrims' Chorus and this quiet room . . . this tomb. . . ."

He slowly went into the bedroom and lay face down on the bed, but even with his eyes shut he saw the blue light of the other room blurring shadows into chairs and tables. Never anything but this room to be furnished now with futile suspicions, a queer dull desire for something his real self rejected, a desire whipped by the insistent memory of a curving white throat.

لم

Vacations were always a problem to Decker, but the present prospect of three months' freedom was unusually frightening. After Teachers' Meeting which was held in the Chemistry Laboratory he saw Louisa Murrell edging toward him and knew he must have answers ready for the current query, "Are you going to the seashore for the summer?" One could say simply, "Indeed no, I must go up to Ann Arbor and work on my M. A.," or there was the perfect answer, "I plan to spend the summer abroad." Decker wished for some wretched farmer cousin who would hide him for the summer, no matter how desolate the place, just so he might vanish from observation, so that the possibility of three months in Dell River would be definitely cancelled.

In April and May teachers were gentler to each other and respectful to Marshall for even though they complained bitterly during the year of Dell River limitations, they were in a panic at the thought of some far-off strange, even smaller post next year or worse yet, no assignment at all. Louisa was not afraid, she knew quite well she had never mattered enough to any superintendent to be discharged, it was always the outspoken, free-thinking sort that had to be fired. She had saved money for years and had almost enough to buy a little place on Cape Cod where she could live quietly and write. She thought about this often but she feared the realization. There she would be a lonely stranger among the dunes with no one to wonder who she was, no one to witness her romantic solitude. And if someone should come to see her in her little house this someone might ask, "How do you spend your days, Miss Murrell, what do you do?" How could she ever hope for courage to answer, "I write all day long. I am a poet, you see, though I do prose quite as easily." She could never come right out and say it even though that was the sole purpose of the venture; however, she saved money and some day when the school dismissed her she would find herself, horror-stricken, on a train bound for that little place on Cape Cod.

Marshall enjoyed those last two months of deference, when the instructors who had been rather superior, as Decker, for instance, during the year, now knuckled under and all but begged for recommendations for next year. He stood at the desk after the teachers left making notes busily on a pad and trying to hear the conversation between Miss Murrell and Decker over by the blackboard, not because he really wanted to eavesdrop or expected to hear anything of moment, but because spying gave him a grateful feeling of authority and power.

"You'll be going abroad, I suppose," said Louisa with a sigh. "How I envy you!"

"Not this year, I'm afraid," Decker answered, frowning a little as if his important affairs were in such a prodigious state of complications that he could scarcely leave them for a pleasure trip. "I planned the trip of course, but—"

"The university, then?" Louisa inquired eagerly. "I went to Normal last summer you know in Michigan."

Decker shook his head.

"No, I shan't bother with any more degrees, I must confess. My mother, of course, will be at her place in the mountains and insists that I join her, but I honestly prefer the sea. . . . Of course my ambition is to own a little place on the coast somewhere— not too far from concerts—"

"Of course!" Miss Murrell agreed.

"—a little place where I could work occasionally, if I should want to do a bit of critical writing, or get into my music once again . . . a little place where I could hear the ocean. . ."

"Cape Cod," said Louisa softly.

"Exactly . . . Then it doesn't matter if I must teach in winter, for at least I have my retreat in summer."

"Yes," said Louisa in a choked voice. "A little place on the Cape where you can hear the ocean."

She looked quickly around to see if Miss Swasey or Miss Emmons were near, for they would be sure to guess why she could not wink back the tears in her eyes. She wouldn't be afraid in that little retreat with Decker. When people asked her what she did she would not need to answer, "I'm a writer," for Decker would be on hand to say, "No, she doesn't write, but I have a friend who does. Starr Donnell, the novelist. My very best friend."

She was frightened that Decker wanted the very same thing she did—it seemed like Fate. She hoped, no matter how intimate and revealing the midnight confidences at The Oaks became she would not tell about this conversation, no matter how much Swasey might tell of men's approaches or Emmons tell of the time she was engaged to the Hazelton widower. She hoped she would be strong enough to lie, saying, "Nothing very thrilling has ever happened to me, girls."

Marshall collected his records and tidied the desk. He smiled remotely at the other two, as if in his benign omnipotence he had heard nothing of their "crush."

"Glad to get away next month, Decker?" he said briskly.

It had to be faced sooner or later so Decker braced himself.

"Certainly not, old man, you forget I'm new to your charming little inland towns. We haven't anything in the East as pleasant as this—a real place for a vacation. I couldn't find a better place for a summer of work—getting my music in order—enlarging on some of my notes—that sort of thing. If I can get out of leaving town I'll be delighted. May run up to my mother's place or take occasional weekends at the Lake but—well, frankly, I'm looking forward to a fine summer right here in the village."

"Well," said Marshall with all his dislike for Decker returning now that Decker had made Dell River so attractive there was no triumph in mentioning his own family plans for a motor trip through Washington, D. C. and Mt. Vernon—he sensed that Decker might be superior even about that.

"I may be here a good deal of the summer," said Louisa suddenly as they went down the dark corridor. "I haven't any plans—nothing definite."

"I see," said Decker absently. He thought of the hot sticky summer nights over the cobbler shop, the blue light burning and the hot droning days and his thoughts all prepared themselves in advance—jealousy over his mother and Rod's family so content in that mountain boarding-house without him—oh quite as if he were dead—and that dumb hurt over Starr and now the endless fretting over Connie.

"I shan't mind it myself at all," he said helping Louisa into her new spring coat. She saw it had paid to get the one with the pretty lining even if it had cost more. "I shan't mind anything, you know, so long as I have my own things about me."

"Your music," sympathized Louisa.

"Yes," said Decker, "my music."

⟳

If you bathed your face in sunrise dew on May day you became beautiful; this was an old saying and every May Mimi meant to do it but no matter how firm her desire the dew was always long gone when she opened her eyes. This year Helen had promised to go out with her to the meadow beyond the river and in case beauty failed to come they could gather mushrooms and violets. It was dark when Mimi wakened and shook Helen, but Helen only muttered, "Let me alone! Don't!" and pulled her blanket over her head protectingly.

"You promised," whispered Mimi. "You can't back out now, Helen, honestly you can't."

Helen could back out of any promise that made her uncomfortable as her sister very well knew and no recriminations could move her. Mimi shook her once again but Helen's long slim body was dissolved into covers, there was no more to grasp here than there was in her entire nature. Depressed, Mimi sat up in bed and faced the fact that if she was to be made beautiful in May dew she must be brave enough to go through the dark meadows alone, for certainly there was no hope of Helen as companion.

Shivering a little she pulled on her stockings and shoes, then drew on her underwear under her thick, cotton nightie as a Sunday school teacher had once taught her to do and finally struggled into the woolen middy suit she had inherited from Helen as her winter school costume. She heard her father's heavy breathing as she tiptoed down the stairs and tried to keep the boards from creaking for there was no explaining this early pilgrimage to her father. The kitchen seemed darkly alive as kitchens do in early morning, as if they kept guard while the house sleeps. The cat brushed against her legs and Mimi took the pail of milk from the outdoor pantry and poured some in a saucer. She found some doughnuts in the breadbox and ate two, stuffing a third in the already crumby pocket of her skirt. She thought, "Of course I don't actually believe in this dew thing but what a grand revenge on Helen if it actually does work out. And Bertha Marshall says it did cure her of freckles."

The tea-kettle lid fell off and clattered to the floor, a pile of muffin tins slid into the sink, a wooden bowl slid off the rack somewhere overhead and spun gaily around the spice shelf, releasing a strong aroma of cinnamon and sweet marjoram. Mimi, sneezing desperately, was almost convinced that there were evil spirits about and certainly all hope of slipping unobserved out of the house was gone for already footsteps could be heard descending the stairs. Her mother appeared in the doorway, her brown hair swinging in rich braids over her faded blue wrapper.

"What is it, Mimi? Are you ill?"

It was too much for Mimi's nerves to bear.

"Bertha said it made her freckles go—I don't believe it but I only wanted to try," she babbled. "Then Helen wouldn't come so

I'm going alone." And then she burst into loud sobs and hid her
face in her hands against the cupboard. "It was just for the fun of
it," she wept. "I don't see why Helen has to spoil it all by backing
out. She'll be good and sorry if I find some mushrooms."

Connie gently patted her shoulder and went to the window.
Day was coming up softly beyond the river. The silver of early
dawn hung over the meadow and tinged the marshy river
banks with unearthly lavender. This early light seemed to come
not from the sky but from the earth, a dull, smoky radiance
exuding from gently opening flowers and wakening grass. The
world was lonely and macabre in this glow, this half-lit world
belonged to strange nightmares, to prehistoric beasts, fantastic
flying things. Connie shuddered and then saw her vague terror
dispelled by a shaft of sudden sunlight.

"Wait, Mimi," she said. "I'll go with you."

She twisted up her braids and pulled on a coat over her
wrapper. They walked swiftly down through the back alley, the
cinders beneath their feet crackling protest in the morning
silence. Houses sagged drearily with sleepers, cold little red
chimneys made a ragged fringe on the pale sky. The winter had
drifted away untidily leaving a scanty patch of stale snow here
and there in hollow stumps beside which violets dared to peep.
When they came to the river the sun burst out, birds shook
themselves and celebrated with shrill joy.

"We'll have to hurry or the dew will be gone," Mimi said
breathlessly. "And it doesn't work except with the first dew."

They found the little dam to cross the shallow river and
made their way over it. The wind shaved the water, whipping
up tiny swirls and ripples as if it were a real river instead of
barely more than a brook. Mimi waited for her mother on the
other side. She remembered her third doughnut and munched
it happily.

"I'm so glad you came," she couldn't help sighing.

They hurried through the meadow across the damp soft
earth until they were out of sight of the village. Mimi ran ahead

COME BACK TO SORRENTO

and impulsively knelt, burying her face in the wet weeds. Connie knelt too and there did seem magic in the tingle of the icy drops on her cheeks for when she lifted her head she felt divinely happy. She sat down on a fallen log near the woods and watched Mimi scurrying around for mushrooms, occasionally finding a stray violet or crocus and dropping it into her out-stretched lap with the mushrooms. Without being conscious of it Connie hummed softly, her body swaying to and fro and then her lungs seemed overwhelmed with the morning air, she opened her mouth wide and sang, hardly knowing what she sang, something she had long ago forgotten but now remembered. This was the way she had always meant to sing, freely, splendidly, but she must never have given hint of such power for Mimi came running up, wide-eyed and dazzled.

From a path in the woods a man appeared. He stood still listening and then took off his hat. When the last note died, birds sang furiously for an instant and then Connie held out her hand for Mimi to start homeward. She was flushed and trembling and had to look twice at the man before she saw it was Busch.

"Lady," said Busch in a choked voice, "I swear to God that's the most beautiful music a man ever heard. I'm telling you the truth and I thank you."

He vanished in the path across the woods and Mimi whispered, "It was—oh, it was beautiful, mother."

Holding her treasures in her lap Mimi balanced herself across the brook once more and Connie followed, her heart thundering in her breast, a thousand voices in her ears saying, "The most beautiful music a man ever heard"—the very words she had always wanted to hear and now due to the magic of the May dew she actually heard them. This was her great premiere, the sunrise and flushing clouds her audience, the grocery man's praise her triumph.

It was enough. Connie's feet scarcely touched earth on their way back to the house and Mimi, in her scurry to keep up with her, scattered a trail of violets and tiny ferns.

࿋

Mr. Busch told Mrs. Busch and Mrs. Busch told Decker. He stood on the front steps of the Busch home and Mrs. Busch talked to him through the gingerly opened parlor door, thrusting her head out and occasionally waving a fat, red forearm, but keeping the rest of her body safely behind the door so that Decker had a delirious impression of a Punch and Judy show, ending with Mrs. Busch's head and shoulders attached to limp sawdust legs being jerked suddenly out of sight. The few inches Mrs. Busch allowed to open permitted a chilling picture of the dreadful parlor behind her, the polychromed pink floor lamp (too good to be used), the gaudy red and pink roses of the carpet, the shiny mahogany-veneered table, the Busch wedding picture— indeed, Decker thought, the whole room looked like a 1905 wedding present and it was. He was deeply relieved that he did not have to sit in it, though he did wonder who in all Dell River was considered worthy of an invitation inside the sacred sill.

"He said, 'Mrs. Busch,' he says to me, 'I never heard anything like it in my life, never, I only wish you could have heard it, he says, coming right out of her throat that way.' "

"Of course! Of course!" Decker nodded and felt so exultant that he wanted to rush at once over to Connie's and congratulate her upon her success quite as if it had been her metropolitan debut.

Mrs. Busch was obliged to open the door a few inches more to receive the bundle of Decker's laundry but she quickly adjusted it again to the proper angle. "As if I were a book agent," thought Decker.

"The way I say is, she may have sounded just as good as the mister says, but do you think that's natural, Professor Decker, for a body to go out singing in the fields at crack o'day? My Honey does it but she's just a child, things like that is natural for a child."

She was alarmed when Decker threw back his head and laughed.

"Well, I only mentioned it to you, her singing, I mean, on account of your being friends and the mister being so tickled with the whole business . . . I didn't see it was so funny as all that . . . I'll get these things back to you Friday."

Decker found the door closed firmly in his face and the next moment the stiff lace curtains of the upper half of the door were parted to permit a fair little girl's face to grimace out at him, thumb her nose and vanish as her mother had done. Decker walked down the front path uncomfortably aware of Honey darting from one window to another to thumb her nose at him. When the gate clicked behind him he heard her singing at the top of her lungs a mocking travesty of "The Spinning Song." Where Mrs. Busch had concealed her own figure he could not guess but he was conscious of being watched and not by the fatuously adoring eyes of an old retainer, either.

"Still, she gets a thrill out of us, I suppose," he thought contentedly. "We probably give her more to puzzle over than all Dell River put together."

He could hear himself telling Connie this after they had first laughed over poor old Mrs. Busch's questioning the sanity of one who sang outdoors instead of at funerals. It was so characteristic of Mrs. Busch to doubt superior intelligence and be proud of her own half-witted daughter. Once Decker had cautiously tried to find out if Mrs. Busch really was unaware of her daughter's deficiency or knew it and was proud of the distinction. Neither was the case. Mrs. Busch felt that she had given birth to a capricious little beauty with the most amazing ways and as unlike as she was superior to every other child in town.

"Isn't she a card?" the mother would fondly exclaim as Honey screamed foul epithets at her little friends. "But that's the way children all are nowadays. And she picks up every little thing she hears, smart as a whip. Oh, she ain't smart in the

usual way, I mean, being still in the third grade and nearly fifteen years old, but I never asked for smartness. I was bright and
what'd it get me? I like a pretty face, I never had one and Mr.
Busch, God knows is no picture, so I said, there ain't nothing I
wouldn't do, Lord, for a pretty little girl. I went to church and
cooked church suppers every week and prayed and when my
baby came people came for miles around to look at her, she was
that pretty. If you work and pray, Mr. Decker, in the end you
get what you want like I did."

Dear, quaint old Busch!

By the time he had turned the corner he was smiling fondly
at the good soul, forgetting the vague sense of inferiority her
daughter's caprices had given him. The little town smelled of
spring, of wet turf, sprouting grass and geraniums. Underfoot
the cinder paths were damply elastic, flowerbeds with white-
pebbled borders were arranged or being arranged on every
lawn in crescents, stars and simple ovals; spades and hoes
leaned against porch lattices and elderly relatives, up to this season of the year nuisances to their families, were happily put to
use white-washing young trees or dropping potatoes in tiny
kitchen gardens. Decker dashed jauntily along the street,
breathing deep of the raw spring air, with a sensation almost of
contentment.

"Not a bad place to live, really," he thought. "Of course if
one were tied here for life it would be frightfully dull, but for a
year or two it's charming. Good friends, my nice little place—I
couldn't have a better one in the Bohemian quarter of any city,
Starr would love the idea of living over a cobbler shop!—I'd
hate to leave it, really!"

Leave it? Where was he going? It was true each fall he
planned to go abroad the following summer, but in the spring
he knew it was impossible, as a winter in New York or Boston
was, too. And as for this coming summer he could do nothing
but stay above the cobbler shop, all vacation money must be
sent to his mother for the mountains, God knew Rod would

never take care of that expense. His mother and Rod seemed further and further away, as if he had never belonged to them, as if he had always belonged to Dell River, the five or six years in that little Virginia town had slid out of his memory. How nicely memory could be made to serve one's happiness, erasing all the things that tended to obliterate the great moments, leaving a Swiss summer with its original colors unmarred even though a dozen summers in American coal towns or hot Midwestern villages came between! Now Decker found himself making room in his mind for a cottage on Cape Cod, the ocean side, he thought. Quite selfishly he took over Louisa's dream cottage. So real did this cottage instantly become that when Laurie Neville stopped her car just then to pick him up he told her at once that he was hoping to get down to his place on the Cape next month.

Miss Manning was driving, her hat stuck on the back of her graying head and one little square-toed boot planted tentatively on the brake. Decker sat in the back of the coupe with Laurie. Laurie's eyes were red, as indeed her nose was too, but the obvious cause of this condition was a mystery to Decker beyond a casual suspicion that Miss Neville probably had a cold. She spoke in a slightly English voice, a product of her foreign schooling and further cause for Dell River men's terror of her, and Miss Manning's accent was distinctively Bostonian so that Decker's own curious accent became, after five minutes' exposure to theirs, more alarmingly Oxfordian than Starr Donnell's had ever dared to be. It was true that even Mr. Marshall, a stickler for good pure Hoosier inflections had caught himself saying "my paunts and vest" in a brief conversation with Miss Neville so that Decker's susceptibility was not to be wondered at.

"I didn't know you had a summer home in the East," said Laurie.

Decker laughed self-consciously. He was never able to feel at ease in an automobile, it still represented aristocracy to him, even though many teachers—even Marshall owned one. To Decker the conversation of people in limousines was that of men in dinner clothes and that of people drinking special wines, it must be rare and studied, a touch theatrical in its cadences; certainly it must deal lightly and wittily with luxurious subjects—vacations, property, opera, decorations, and all material beauties. In the comfortable purple cushioned seat of Laurie's car it actually seemed to him he was a man of property and position.

"The place is not exactly in my hands yet, it is true," he admitted. "I'm not satisfied at the price they're asking."

"Where is it?" Miss Manning asked, without turning her head and without really wanting an answer since she could never drive and listen at the same time.

"Wellfleet," said Decker, capturing the name from somewhere far back. in his memory. "Of course, the real drawback is that I'm expected abroad in June. My friends are there—Starr Donnell, the novelist—"

"Yes," said Miss Manning.

"I sometimes think," said Decker musingly while the little houses of Dell River appeared one by one in the window of the car, each one modestly inviting his mind to return to reality. "I sometimes think it would be wiser to give up the plan for the cottage, give up Europe too, and stay here in this little town and get to know it. With my work I've never had a chance to study the place, get the feel of it, don't you know."

"Don't stay," said Laurie abruptly. "Go where there's music and people who aren't afraid of you."

"Laurie thinks Dell River is afraid of intelligent people," said Miss Manning in the cheerful, hard voice she used to balance growing hysteria in her friend. "Paris would be ideal, of course."

Decker flicked ashes of his cigarette out the window, bowed briefly to Louisa Murrell just coming down the front steps of The Oaks.

"I'm afraid I'm something of a snob, Miss Neville," he said. "I can't bear travel except under first-class conditions. I must have my little luxuries, you know, and I can't do the way my friends there would expect me to. So I'll be perfectly contented here in Dell River. I've always wanted to investigate those woods over there and walk out beyond those hills by the Nursery."

"There would be the festival at Salzburg," said Laurie Neville. "All the things you love . . ." She suddenly leaned toward him. "Let me take you. It would be so easy for me to do. Let me . . . I assure you we would make it as comfortable for you as you'd like. . . . Do let me do that for you, Professor Decker."

Decker was stunned. He had no answers ready for kindness or for reality. His words, like Mrs. Benjamin's, were for protection from people, not for communication with them. He met in the little crescent-shaped driver's mirror the quizzical eye of Miss Manning and its gentle cynicism braced him, it seemed so sardonically certain of his greedy acceptance.

"My dear lady," he answered with a little laugh, "if I really wanted to go abroad I'd go—it isn't a question of money, oh dear no!"

"But you said—" Laurie flushed and her lip trembled.

"Don't misunderstand me," Decker said with a wide flourish of his cigarette. "Fortunately I'm not dependent on teaching as poor old Marshall is, for instance, and if I really wanted to travel—! I was only trying to be judicious in my spending, that was all. Sorry I gave you the wrong impression."

Laurie looked mutely out of the other window and Miss Manning drove hastily around the Square and stopped the car before the cobbler shop.

"It would have been nice to have you with us, Laurie thought," said Miss Manning as Decker got out. "One needs a man travelling.

Decker bowed over Laurie's outstretched hand.

"I wish I could be there to take you around among my friends," he said. "Fascinating people. I miss them constantly. Artists—then there's Ilsa Darmster and Starr—"

Laurie drew her hand away and dabbed savagely at her eyes with a handkerchief. Miss Manning silently released the brake and the two women drove home in silence.

Decker dropped in on Gus, feeling as exhilarated as if he had just returned from actual visits to Paris and his Wellfleet house. Seeing Gus gloomily bent over the work-table he called out, "I hear your wife has a wonderful voice—the whole town's talking about it. They've waked up at last."

"Maybe," said Gus. He raised his eyes to Decker and said bleakly, "'I had the doctor for her this time. It's in her chest. She had a hemorrhage this morning."

꒰

Gus put a day-bed in the front living room downstairs so that Connie could watch people out of her window during the long days of convalescence. At night Mimi slept on the dining-room sofa so that she could wait on her mother if anything happened. Helen was frightened at first into keeping house without a murmur, and once she broke into hysterical sobs at her mother's bedside because at school they said it was tuberculosis. For Dell River the word was like leprosy, and nice people did not have it. After a few weeks the business of getting the family breakfast, even with Mimi's help, restored Helen to her normal resentment and by Junior Prom time with no one to help her make her party dress, Helen was convinced the whole thing was part of the family's determination to ruin her life. When she came into the front room to take away Connie's supper tray she always pulled down all the shades and arranged the curtains carefully so that her own privacy on the porch might be maintained. Sometimes Helen studied her mother's face shrewdly to see if she could detect any guile there, for Helen wouldn't have been surprised to learn that her entire family deliberately peeked through walls at her whenever she had a boyfriend. That was the trouble with this family—a girl had no privacy and now that all the house sofas were in practical use a girl might as well have no home at all.

Mimi felt embarrassed about Helen for the sake of her mother and Professor Decker and Miss Murrell—none of the lovely, gracious, far-off people they discussed would ever act as Helen did. But when she hinted as much to Helen she realized that however she felt over her sister was nothing to her sister's humiliation over her. It appeared that the high-school crowd disapproved of Mimi.

"You might as well walk in from Bluff Corners every day carrying your lunch-basket with hay in your hair," Helen informed her in exasperation. "It's all over school every time a boy tries to kiss you, you scream—"

"I never!" Mimi was scarlet with shame.

"You did so. And they only do it then for a joke to see if you'll scream louder," Helen went on. "You don't know as much as I did when I was ten and here you are—nearly fourteen. You can imagine how I feel having everyone talk about you—calling you a sap!"

So Mimi was crushed with the knowledge that the only crime was to be a sap and in this respect Helen looked upon her family and their friends as utter criminals. When the girls would come home from school with the Marshall boy in tow Mimi would skip along beside the other two, trying to give the watching villagers the impression that they were just three school friends but most of the time neither young Marshall or Helen spoke to Mimi and at the front door Helen would say peremptorily as if, Mimi thought indignantly, she were a baby—and right before a boy, too, "Go on in and fix supper. Don doesn't want to have to talk to the whole family."

Mimi could not help thinking of the world of politeness and pretense to which her mother and Professor Decker belonged. "People ought to pretend," she thought, "Don ought to pretend he came to see the whole family even if he didn't."

Connie was no longer ill but lay quietly day and night waiting for Decker's afternoon calls, marking off the Saturdays and Sundays when he was there all afternoon. She cried softly when she was alone, thinking of how good Gus was, how kind Mrs. Busch was, how very kind everyone in the world was. She could hear the girls quarreling over the housework but it seemed to her to arise from the fine spirits of youth and not from any ill temper.

Heretofore she had loved best the night hours, the drowsy modulation from wakefulness to sleep when she painted her own life in richer colors, but now she had all day to dream. Her body, no longer in pain but drained of all energy and purpose, demanded nothing from her, so fancies flowed through her mind lightly, warmed her veins, filled her with perpetual excitement and a sense of approaching joy. The sound of Decker's quick steps on the porch was almost unbearably thrilling—ah, what things she had to tell him today! Little childhood impressions tenderly resurrected, new meanings read into suddenly remembered advice from Manuel, a compliment from the nuns about her flair for musical criticism. With no present and only a vague happy confidence in the future she had nothing to do but elaborate upon a recreated past until even her senses seemed not to respond to the sensations of the moment so overburdened were they with their remembered reactions. If Decker was late in arriving Connie would talk to Mimi or if possible to Mrs. Busch on these fascinating shadings in her past. One day she thought of the strange way fate justifies itself after many years.

"Supposing my grandfather had allowed me to go on with a career," she said to Mrs. Busch. "Then on the evening of my debut I had this very attack! How humiliating to have my career ruined on the very eve after perhaps months of hard preparation—how much better never to have gotten into it at all! Because now, though I won't be able to sing at all for awhile, at least I have no manager to scold me, I don't *have* to sing!"

"Yes, and you shouldn't talk so much either," said Mrs. Busch practically. "You save your breath, let me tell you."

"But it only shows how wisely everything works out in life, Mrs. Busch, don't you see?" Connie explained eagerly.

"Yes, I know," Mrs. Busch responded briefly and returned to the kitchen to finish her washing. Now that she was giving two or three mornings a week to the Benjamins, their house reeked perpetually of steaming soapsuds, damp woolens and ammonia. Connie longed to be outdoors in the fragrant early summer air and even though the doctor summoned from the big hospital at Greentown through Miss Neville recommended the outdoors Gus knew better and was certain fresh air was death to a weak chest. So Connie lay propped up on pillows in the front room, her eyes wistfully watching the leaves thickening on the porch vine until they had made a glistening green barrier between her and the street, and the sunlight appeared merely in tiny triangular apertures through the leaves, unable to send more than a few weak rays into the sick-room.

The day after Commencement when Decker had so many gay stories to tell, including that of the renewal of his own contract, he could not bear to sit in this sad sunless room, so without consulting Gus he arranged the cot in the backgarden and helped Connie out there. After the weeks indoors the garden seemed unbelievably beautiful and her heart choked her. Gus, usually painstaking of his garden, had been paralyzed by her illness into neglect so that tulips fought for survival among the ragweeds, and hyacinths, stunted by crowding strangers, cowered together like little girls in party dresses frightened of big boys; the tall larkspur had been beaten down by the rain and the brilliant blue ruined blossoms peeped through matted clover and sourgrass. The vines had died on the summer house and it looked brightly ugly in undisguised saffron paint, its broken rail and crippled bench no longer concealed by kind Nature. But to Connie this stretch of ground, so long desired, was perfect, she dared not at first risk the ecstatic shock of lifting her face to the wide June sky and when she did the light puffs of clouds seemed as festival as a birthday cake, the very day a jewel set in celestial blue seemed a gift from someone who loved her deeply.

Propped up on cushions, her faded silk scarves tied loosely about her hair and throat, she looked more beautiful than Decker had ever seen her. As he talked to her sometimes the blue transparency of her long hands adjusting their blankets made him frightened as if this illness was real, not just a pretty little accident to vary the monotony of their lives. People do get really ill—they die—but not us, not anyone like us! . . . He pulled the broken wicker chair from the summer house and placed it near her to get a view of the river though the modest little stream was obscured now by tangled bushes, all that could be seen from the garden was an ancient locust tree that dropped thick fragrant blossoms lazily into the water and with every breeze released a heavy, tantalizing perfume.

"In one way it's lucky you never went on with your career," Decker said. "Supposing this illness had come on the eve of an important concert engagement—"

"I know! Exactly what I said to Mrs. Busch," exclaimed Connie, marvelling again that Decker should have her identical thoughts. "Doesn't it make you frightened to see the way Fate works out? There might even be some meaning in my being in Dell River instead of—well, say Indianapolis—or Iowa—or Flint, Michigan!"

"In my coming here, too," added Decker. "And that reminds me I'll be staying here this summer. Fuss about with my music and brush up a bit on the piano. So I shan't be able to go to the mountains or shore as I rather planned."

"Too bad," sighed Connie and then had a terrified moment trying to realise what would happen if Decker had had to leave for the summer—or for good. What meaning would her days have then, how could one live without some interested listener to give importance to the little details of one's routine? Pain had been bearable, even exciting, because it was a new experience to be described to Decker and thus tenderly shared. Without the assurance that sensation was impossible, without a later audience in mind pain could only be a barren avenue to death.

Louisa came around the corner of the house as Decker was telling of his yearnings for a place on the Cape. She wore the blue printed foulard dress and blue glazed straw that Dell River had last summer associated with Laurie Neville, but in accepting Laurie's cast-offs Louisa had the conviction that they looked far smarter on a woman of her own type so that the town would not recognize them on her at all. "And what if they do?" inquired Miss Emmons who was indeed envious of being too large for cast-offs herself. "They know you're not so rich you can refuse clothes—if you were you wouldn't be teaching here, would you?" This was the sort of thing that irritated Louisa beyond endurance, this bald facing of unfortunate facts. One couldn't even say—"Dear me—another gray hair!" without Miss Emmons laughing shrilly, "Well, good Lord, what do you expect at thirty-five!" From these good-natured interchanges Louisa emerged bruised and hurt, frantically eager for the soothing contact with Mrs. Benjamin and Decker. Here, of all places, no one would remember Laurie Neville's old clothes or observe the sad signals of middle-age, here in this magic circle one was known by words and Louisa's word was "poetry."

She blushed seeing Decker lounging in the chair smoking, there was always something alarmingly intimate in meeting him out of the classroom, for one thing he wore glasses in school and these spectacles were a stern barrier to human interchange; with this uniform removed they became only human, almost, Louisa thought—naked, no longer Professor and

Teacher but two gentle creatures, defenseless against the world, orphaned of blackboard and spectacles. Louisa felt such a rush of protective warmth for Decker that it seemed incredible he could himself be unconscious of their bond. Certainly there was nothing but formal gallantry in his manner as he rose, clicked his heels and offered her his chair.

He sat at the foot of Connie's bed. "I'm going to be Miss Neville's guest at their place on the Lake this summer," Louisa said the instant Decker allowed her to speak. "I was afraid I'd have to stay at The Oaks—except for my usual two weeks at my sister's in Monessen—but now I can spend a whole week on the shore. A real vacation!"

"Splendid!" said Decker kindly, not really caring.

"Miss Manning said Laurie wanted you to go abroad with them as a sort of escort," Louisa went on with an inquiring inflection. "I can't see why you don't go, I really can't, Professor Decker."

Connie put her hand slowly over her heart, the pain that shot through her was too acute to be only mental. Afterward she wondered why the reactions to an emotion should come before her mind had even registered the fact.

Decker ground his cigarette into the earth with his heel.

"After all, dear Louisa, I'm not a tourists' guide," he said patronizingly. "I think Miss Neville understands that. Besides I'm not at all sure I care about leaving America this summer. France in summer with all the tourists—oh no, I don't think summer is the time for foreign travel."

"A dreadful time!" agreed Connie breathlessly. "I don't blame you!"

"If I went I should want to spend the winter," mused Decker.

"It was kind of Miss Neville, I thought," Louisa timidly suggested but both Connie and Decker looked blankly at her as if the kindness had been on Decker's side in merely listening to the proposition. Thinking of a year abroad Decker's face became set, he was silent, and Connie looked at the locust tree yonder, her heart beating frantically . . . Decker to be gone a year? . . . Laurie Neville arranging all this so a charming dream should become a nightmare of reality . . . Decker gone. August—September—October—without Decker . . . She pulled the blanket up about her shoulders, cold with fear. In the silence Louisa Murrell pulled a little book out of her bag.

"This is the one you asked me to read again—the Blake one—" she moistened her lips—"the one about the Garden of Love.

> "'I laid me down upon a bank
> Where love lay sleeping.
> I heard among the bushes dank
> Weeping, weeping.'"

Decker's eyes left the snowcapped Jungfrau he was seeing beyond the river and met Connie's as the gaze of two drowning people might meet above the waves—farewell to me, the eyes said, oh farewell. . . . Louisa coughed and went on—

> "'Then I went down to the heath and the wild
> To the thistles and thorns of the waste—'"

Why had Laurie Neville, Connie wondered passionately, made Decker that offer, why unless she wanted him? She was free and wealthy. She could marry him. She could support him forever in Paris where he would be happy. A spasm of hate for Gus came over Connie, it was Gus' fault, standing like a stone wall, like her grandfather's stone wall ready to crush anything beautiful. . . . She closed her eyes, tired out from the unaccustomed feeling, but when she opened them again Decker was looking at her and he seemed suddenly very little and shabby and forlorn, a stray begging to be released from its chain for pity's sake. . . .

"I'd better go in," she whispered faintly. "You and Louisa can stay here—"

"We wouldn't dream of it," said Decker quickly. He took her arm but their flesh shrank curiously from each other's, rejected the contact as yellow and white flesh rebel against each other.

Connie thought dizzily, "I must find Tony, I must try some other way to find Tony."

Drowning, drowning . . .

"I'll leave the book for you," Louisa suggested after she had fixed the living-room couch once more for Connie. "You always loved that one so much. I think it should be set to music, don't you, Professor Decker?"

"Yes," said Decker. He was afraid to stay in the room now and looked slyly beyond Louisa as if he expected doors to lock themselves and forbid flight. He did not want to look at Connie but it could not be helped. How shockingly naked her arm looked curved under her head! Some women could wear a dozen wrappings and still their eyes would be undressed, he thought, fighting this sensation of chains tightening, the trap closing in on him, definitely, ominously. He fought the veiled word in his mind, beat it back into the darkness as a monster foe who must not kill that precious toy, the magic world of Decker, the genius, and Madame Benjamin, artiste. . . . The word shone almost slyly in Mrs. Benjamin's brown eyes, it lay in the curve of her arm, it hovered in polite ambush in Louisa's puzzled frown as she looked from Decker to the sick woman. Like a masked beggar in an opera it crouched in shadows ready at the final curtain to drop mask and rags and stand revealed in shattering splendor.

"I'll walk to The Oaks with you, Louisa," he said. "We may be tiring her, and she mustn't get tired, the doctor said."

Both Connie and Decker smiled gratefully at Louisa as if her pale presence had for once fully justified her. Connie patted the little books on the table.

"It's so good to have this. When one can't keep at one's singing, poetry is a real refuge."

"You'll be well enough for the Chautauqua concerts," Louisa encouraged her. "We can go together, unless of course it comes while I'm at the lake. Those summer concerts are sometimes excellent."

Professor Decker smiled and was able to meet Connie's glance with an amused smile.

"Of course they are," said Connie kindly. "Especially when you have so little chance at real music."

"So many Dell River people have never heard anything else," Louisa apologized hastily. "Naturally to a professional musician they wouldn't seem very good. I only thought—"

"Oh Mrs. Benjamin and I are both enormously grateful for even an echo of 'Il Trovatore,'" said Decker benignly. "Beggars can't choose, you know. And sometimes a real talent turns up in just such places."

"A Tyler Stewart," said Louisa. "That type."

Connie flushed and Decker frowned. Louisa, ready now to dawdle over her departure since they seemed to be getting into a discussion of their favorite sort, was surprised to find Decker holding the screen open for her. Connie said goodbye weakly and turned her face to the wall. The wheels of her brain were too tired to deal with the immense word, she could only follow carefully with her eyes the formal pattern of the wallpaper, stiff rows of brown bell-shaped blossoms twined in faded yellow leaves. The failing sunlight filtered through the window vines, the back garden was still there with the trampled larkspur, Connie mused, and the locust tree, but Louisa and Decker were on the outside with real gardens while she must lie here indoors afraid to think. She must not think of Laurie Neville or of what life would be without Decker . . . she mustn't think of what might happen—impossibly enough—if this weakness of hers grew worse instead of better, if for her summer would be only the distant croaking of the bullfrogs, the fluttering of humming birds in the porch vines, if for her gardens would be a conventionalized lotus on wallpaper.

"If I only were allowed to sing a little," she thought fretfully, "then nothing would matter."

༈

For ten years Commencement Day had been for Decker an empty day of blank sky and pointless sunshine, a gay mask for a great Nothing; a day of echoing auditoriums, bleating of young voices, a screen of noise through which his despairing ear detected the dreary monotone of another year exactly like the last. A day of unexpectedly fond farewells to other teachers and young men as one realized that hollow as these relations had been, they were at least warmer than those impending. Decker found himself clinging to Louisa's hand in the little station by the Nursery greenhouses, as if the few weeks she was to be gone were as important to him as they were to her.

"I'll visit my sister's family for two weeks and then go to Miss Neville's cottage," Louisa explained in a high excited voice. "It won't be anything thrilling of course, nothing more than staying in Dell River—"

"But it's the going away," Decker interrupted wistfully. "It's the change. And besides there won't be anyone left in the Village."

"Except Mrs. Benjamin," said Louisa. "It's really a good thing you're being here with her sick. It will be so nice for her. You can talk over so many things in three months."

Decker saw the summer months approaching as three gay dancers, hands clasped, closing in on him, drawing him tighter towards Connie until there would be no space between them, no escape; fantastically the dancers grew larger, their flying draperies swelled to huge dark clouds enormous, suffocating, no spoken sonnet could break this dreadful magic nor the resolute fortissimo of a favorite Prelude. Louisa was moved by his

weary, pale face, and looked hard at a truck laden with brilliant
flowers emptying its frivolous burden into the dingy maw of a
freight-car, she winked away tears thinking that this rare,
delightful man was actually sorry for her departure. She gripped
his hand passionately and then as abruptly dropped it. She
would do anything in the world for him, she thought, anything—anything. If he were sick, he did look so frail, she would
take care of him, she would feed him delicate broths made by
her own hands—she was a wretched cook in reality, nevertheless for him she would excel, she would hold his sad charming
head against her frail breast, she would write great tomes
which would be sold to motion picture companies for millions
and with this she would surround him with the grandeur he
missed, she would scrub, unless perhaps something really needed
scrubbing, a hopeless business, then, as a matter of fact. . . . She
wanted nothing from him, nothing, she thought, but to suffer
hardships for him, to have her whole body tired with work for
him, and when she was so spent with sacrifices for him that she
could only smile a frozen blessing on him from her coffin then
he would notice her and say, "Dear little Louisa! No one was
ever so good to me. No one!"

Then this bold fancy alarmed her, she fumbled in her purse
for tickets fearing that these flying images were imprinted
shamelessly on her face for Decker to read. Decker's thoughts
however were so far away from her that he started when the
distant whistle of an engine brought him back to the slight little
creature at his side.

"A few weeks with your family, eh," he repeated her
words. "A few weeks of being spoiled, of course, but it will do
you good. You should have a little pampering."

"Thank you," said Louisa with a hysterical impulse to
laugh wildly. Pampering? In the brief interval of watching the
far-off smoke materialize into approaching engine she pictured the weeks of "pampering" which in all the years of
vacations with her family had varied so little. The small house

which her arrival threw uncomfortably out of joint, the dingy, busy little town with its perpetual soot cloud from the factories, the house smelling of sour milk and baby clothes, the endless whimpering of the latest baby as obbligato to the staccato arguments of Eleanor and Dale, their affectionate bossing of old Mr. Murrell who only asked to be left quietly alone . . . Louisa already prepared the defensive smile with which she would answer Dale's genial "Well, back again, Louisa! And not married yet, I'll be bound! Well, never mind, while there's life there's hope, ha ha, as the old man says!" Each year—seven on this very platform—she had tried to strengthen herself before she got on the train so that her return to her family would be triumphal rather than the sad homecoming of the defeated, but the complacency of her sister's family always disarmed her. No use pointing out to Eleanor or Dale the advantages of her single career, they, even in their quarrels and economies, were certain of their own enviable position, their smiling pity made her discontented, their proud flaunting of connubial intimacies made an old maid of her. Pampering . . . Two months of squeezing out of her the last vestige of vanity, affectionately demonstrating how pitiful were her personal charms, how inadequate her gifts, how much they loved her for being so sweetly inferior to them, until on her departure she wept to think of leaving this tender patronage for a world more austerely just to such defections as hers.

"This year at least I can hold on to the idea of visiting Laurie Neville," she consoled herself. "I never had any place to go before except other relatives', the convention, or summer school. And they can't do much to me in four weeks, they're rather sure to be impressed with such a grand invitation. Dale is stupid but he knows a place like Belmeer Lake is pretty swell. That will keep him down . . . No, this year it will be better, the way it was that first year after the war when I was the only one in the family who'd been over . . . They thought I was wonderful then. I almost was, too—with all of them believing it . . ."

"I wish," said Decker picking up her bags so masterfully that Louisa was sorry the other teachers weren't there to see, "that I could join my own family this year but once in three years is all I've ever done. . . . It's impossible, anyway, to do one's work with a family fussing over one."

"I'm sure yours spoils you," said Louisa.

Decker raised his shoulders modestly.

"An older son always is over-rated . . . I realize that, but how could I tell my mother I'm not the genius she thinks I am?"

Louisa wanted to say, "Oh, but you are a genius, you are, no matter what you actually do, you're a great man!" but there was no time. She found her seat in the train and when she wanted to say some special word to him, something that would spread out delicately in his memory after she left recalling her to him as a definite fragrance might, she saw such a cool, politely remote smile on his face that her own warmth was checked; she had the startled conviction that no matter how deftly she built farewell words into a bridge across their separation it would signify not the slightest thing to him, she might as well just say "Goodbye" and forget him as easily as she herself would be forgotten. This fear chilled her but as the train slid out the old tenderness returned. She rubbed a clean triangle on the window-pane and watched his slight but, she felt, arresting figure swagger across the station tracks, his thick walking stick synchronizing so neatly with his stride that to Louisa at least here was masculine power at its finest. Straining her eyes she watched him as he swung across the station green and turned buoyantly at the corner in the direction of Mrs. Benjamin's cottage.

꒰

Laurie brought her doctor to see Mrs. Benjamin after Gus had told Miss Manning in the shop of the danger.

"Of course I'll see him," Connie had said when Miss Neville hesitatingly proposed her specialist from the city hospital. Miss Neville had been afraid Connie might consider it an officious suggestion but Connie assumed she was doing Miss Neville a favor in accepting. She had reached the stage where perpetual languor would be hard to surrender, what would she do with a return of vitality? In health she had little excuse for slurring her household duties, for being an indifferent mother and wife. There was relief in being absolved from domestic responsibilities, a forlorn joy in being set apart even by misfortune.

Laurie Neville had seldom called on her before but now the little gray roadster often stopped before the Benjamin house and Laurie, usually accompanied by Miss Manning, sat in the tumbled garden with a gracious but wan hostess. Laurie talked of operas, of concerts she had heard last year in Pittsburgh or New York, of this or that new conductor just over from Holland, of a Viennese singer who had dazzled New York, and Connie would nod, smiling, as if all these matters were old news to her so close was she to the real center of music that she needed to be told nothing, the progress of music was not to be marked by newspapers but by her specially appointed sensory system. When Laurie left musical weeklies or magazine clippings with her Connie barely glanced at them, these guides were for the outsider and uninitiated, there was nothing she needed to be told. Moreover, the world these journals described was at no point tangent to the Decker and Benjamin world. It was a world of trade talk, catalogues of definite names and works and this was not the music that sang for Connie and Decker. Connie felt gently superior to such outsiders and believed that Laurie called on her in a deferential spirit.

The day the city doctor came it rained and Connie waited in the living room, dressed but exhausted with the fever which seemed never to leave her. To her surprise Gus closed the shop in order to be home when the visitors came and he sat by the door gloomily looking from Connie to the street. He was only a few years older than she but in the last year he had shrunk into a bent hunched little old man, bright blue eyes glaring morosely under shaggy graying brows. He would look like this for the next thirty years, perhaps, bending over more ever so slightly each year, arriving at seventy a grizzled Wagnerian dwarf.

"But I'm getting better, Gus," Connie protested. "There's no use your staying here. All he will do is give me a tonic or diet and there's no need your being here for that."

"I don't know," said Gus. "He might say you had to go away."

"Go away?" exclaimed Connie. "But why should I? I couldn't get any more rest than I get here. The girls and Mrs. Busch do everything for me ... Why should he send me away?"

Gus pulled at his pipe silently and watched the street. It was raining lightly and steadily, the vine leaves glistened and fluttered in the fresh eastern wind, a wet robin perched on the porch rail shaking his feathers luxuriously, two little girls ran squealing past, their light frocks drenched. The smell of wet nasturtium leaves came to Connie's nostrils and she wished at once for Decker who would catch this bitter fragrance at the moment she did and one of them would say, "Nasturtium is really the flower for rainstorms—better than violet, I think," and then the other would very likely say, "More earthy."

She was growing more and more weary of the hours when he could not be there. Since her life centered so completely around him it was ridiculous that they should have so little time together. Two or three hours a day—it was nothing when the other twenty-one were spent vacantly wishing for the meeting or fondly spreading out past discussions in mind as line drawings to be colored at leisure with one's own crayons. It had been many months since her conversations with Gus had concerned anything but his tenant, though it was hard to draw anything but monosyllabic answers from him. Had he heard Decker's piano lately? was it a concert piece or something for the school chorus? or did it sound hesitating and broken as if he might be composing it himself? Gus would shrug his shoulders. He had heard the piano—wasn't that answer enough? And had he heard voices upstairs, had Miss Neville called, if she had did she bring flowers or papers resembling new music as she used sometimes to do? Connie was impatient with Gus for paying so little heed to the details of Decker's life, though she knew in a few hours Decker himself would tell her all these things, decorating each point as if it were an after-dinner story. It delighted her, however, to be able to surprise him as he entered her house with, "Ah, so you did go riding with the Marshalls after all! You see how scandal spreads!"

Decker would smile, surprised and flattered that his busy social life should be the talk of the town. One day Mimi reported the great news that he had been seen in Mills' music store purchasing one of the new portable gramophones and Connie was able to gayly accuse him of this shocking extravagance when he called that same afternoon.

"But how did you know?" he demanded, his face clouding. "I told Mills not to tell you. It was to be a surprise for you."

"For me?" Connie raised herself on her elbow to stare at him. "You got it for me—oh, my dear Blaine!"

"I thought we could take it to my place when you got better," he explained, "but keep it here the rest of the time."

The gift was so important to her, so close to her heart that she could not thank him at first. Later when Gus brought her a record—a gay Bavarian dance tune played on an accordion, the instrument Gus had once tried to learn, the dark thought struck Connie that she must be going to die to meet with such a conspiracy of kindness. It was not like Decker to do more than wish for such luxuries as this, and she could not recall ever receiving a gift from Gus beyond a great clock for the house on one birthday and at Christmas an occasional new petticoat or woolen kimono, never anything to indicate a knowledge of her real tastes.

"I must have some disease they won't tell me about," she thought, frightened of death already, a long, black wait for Decker it seemed to her, shuddering. It was not the picture of herself, silent, shut in the earth that made her cry aloud with fright, but the thought of how many times Decker's footsteps would pass her and she would not know, how many things he would have to tell her and she would not hear. The quick familiar rap-rap on the loose screen door on summer nights, the cigarette smoke curling in the air after he left, that gentle modulation from presence to absence; the perpetual feeling of suspense, waiting for him to call, and now that he was here waiting for tomorrow's visit. Connie wept for the death, not of herself, but of all these things . . . She saw Gus' staying home for the doctor a further dark proof, and scarcely dared ask for Mimi and Helen lest it prove they too were staying home from their planned picnic. She watched Gus' silent, inexpressive face and was heartened to see no sign of worry there in spite of the evidence of his actions, she heard the girls at last moving furniture about upstairs and thought, "Of course they didn't have the picnic because it was raining." And if this were so serious wouldn't Decker have been here instead of playing chess with the German barber? Of course, Decker would not fail her, for one afternoon if she were in danger, and at once his defection today which had disappointed her so much, seemed the most delightful gay gesture he had ever made. He was not here— therefore her fear was preposterous.

"You say Professor Decker was in the barber shop when you came?" Connie asked Gus to make sure and when Gus nodded she exclaimed, "I'm so glad he couldn't come."

Gus removed his pipe.

"Well I should think so," he said with a depth of honest feeling. "You've been too nice to that young man, Connie. Just because he rents our place is no sign you got to keep him from getting homesick. I should think you would get tired hearing him talk."

"I didn't mean that," Connie laughed a little.

"What then?" Gus inquired, vaguely angry with her as he was with his daughters and women in general for having secret laughter. Seeing that Connie had no answer but lay there smiling at the window he resumed his pipe and the gloomy wait for sight of the Neville car. Her fright had vanished and now she thought it would not be long before she was completely herself. She traced with her forefinger the pattern of lotus on the wall, then turned, still smiling, to watch the rain trembling on the window-pane.

When Laurie finally appeared with the doctor Gus stood awkwardly in the doorway of the living room looking so morose that Connie was embarrassed.

"My husband is a coward about doctors," she explained to the visitors. "He thinks they're as final as undertakers, so please tell him I'm getting better. Anyone else could see it."

The doctor was a heavy-jowled dark man with tangled graying eyebrows, his rimless spectacles seemed designed to protect the world from his steely relentless black eyes. It was incredible that women should fancy a caress might stir momentary tenderness in these eyes, yet some believed in the miracle. Laurie Neville stood beside Gus trying to talk to him but her glances kept straying hungrily toward the doctor.

There seemed nothing extraordinary to Connie in Miss Neville's interest in her health. After all were they not the two leading figures in Dell River cultural life and though their previous contacts had been only pleasantly accidental, Connie would have said they understood each other. The visits from Miss Neville's doctor seemed more of a social call than a professional one. She was annoyed at Gus' silent refusal to offer them any of his wine, to make any hospitable gesture.

"You know this attack has been so inconvenient for me, Doctor," she said brightly. "I had planned to do a great deal of work this summer."

"Out of the question," said Doctor Arnold bruskly. "Let someone else take care of the house."

"I meant my singing," Connie explained gently. "I've been rather lax with my practicing—there's so little to encourage me in the Village as you can see. . . . But I really intended working at it this summer. You know, Doctor, I was started on a musical career years ago but—well, things happened to stop me." She shrugged sadly. "Perhaps I wouldn't have been strong enough to stand that life."

"Probably not," answered the doctor absently. He ignored Laurie's beseeching look and studied Connie thoughtfully.

"I sang before Morini. He said—'The throat of an artist,'" Connie went on. "I had no one to help me so—Even now I live only for my music. I suppose I might take it up professionally once again if it comes to that."

"Doctor, she ought not to talk so much," Gus broke in roughly. "I've told her."

"That's true," said the doctor. "All unnecessary exertion is bad."

Connie flushed deeply. She saw so few strangers she wanted to make an event of this occasion but Gus' rudeness had spoiled it. She saw the doctor preparing to go and tried frantically to think of ways to detain him. It was such a relief to find someone so interested in her work—at least that was the way she construed his absorbed attention. Gus must understand that a woman with a career is not a mere wife, but an artist first and foremost. She felt her eyelids burning and futile excitement mounting in her as it did every afternoon as if something unbearably delightful was about to happen. The succeeding letdown each day was increasingly hard to endure, and by her bedtime she was trembling with exhaustion. Gloomy dreams would assemble vaguely in her mind, dreams of pain or sorrow which made her sob and moan in her sleep. She saw no reason to speak of this state of mind to Doctor Arnold but his hard black eyes seemed to read it all from her tired face.

The doctor and Gus went into the dining room out of hearing. Connie was quiet, trying to collect her energy for a last plea

for him to stay, just to take the visit from its almost brutally
professional tone. She smiled at Laurie Neville who had drawn
a chair to the side of her bed but was looking past her toward
the two men with intent interest. Connie thought with surprise
that Miss Neville was an exceedingly handsome woman, so
striking with her vivid eyes and coloring as to seem almost
exotic. She gripped Connie's arm suddenly and nodded toward
the dining-room.

"Isn't he marvellous, Mrs. Benjamin?" she whispered.
"When I watch him talking to a patient, measuring him with
those eyes, my heart almost stops. Actually I feel myself melting
away. I think—'How strong he is, how completely sane—how
sure!' I could die of admiration. Sometimes when I go to him
with all sorts of things wrong with me he tells me—just by a
glance at me—exactly what's the matter. Then of course he
thinks as Manning does that I'm hysterical, but it isn't that.
Really it isn't that. Is it hysterical to worship strength, do you
think, Mrs. Benjamin?"

Connie was surprised by the unexpected rush of confidence
and by Miss Neville's strangely intense manner.

"Have you known him so long?" was all she could think
to ask.

"Seven years."

Laurie watched his big broad back as she whispered and
occasionally she would glance out toward the rainy street as if
she expected Miss Manning to appear and march her off as if
she were a child staying too long at the birthday party.

"I went to him first for my father's last illness. Then I was
often sick but he is so busy now that I can't get him to come
over to Dell River except for other people's illnesses. Never to
my house for dinner—not even when I ask his wife, too."

She rose abruptly and went to the porch door, her nervous
fingers beating upon the screen. The low voices of the men in
the other room dropped a word or phrase clean-cut on the air and
Connie tried to piece them together as fragments of a picture

puzzle. "Mountains"—"recurrent attacks"—"expenses"— . . .
The words were as puzzling as Laurie's curious actions and her
fears of earlier in the day had worn her out so much that she was
now too tired to worry. Her eyelids fluttered dryly over her hot
eyeballs, she only wanted things to be clear and simple, these
furtive whispers and shadowy corners defeated her.

"Doesn't he make you feel strong—just his being here?"
Laurie demanded huskily. She returned to the chair beside the
bed and leaned over it. "Sometimes Manning makes me feel the
same way—but not much any more. Have you ever thought
how few people there are who can make you feel completely
unafraid? They terrify me—alone or in crowds. Their eyes say
—'Who are you—what is your excuse?' I have no excuse for
existing. Nothing. If I want to be kind their eyes accuse me
again. 'So you want to bribe us into liking you, make us admit
you have some excuse.' . . . Before I was sick I used to travel
alone, dine alone in restaurants, talk to no one on shipboard. At
my table would often be some famous person I would give my
soul to talk to. But I was afraid. Their eyes made me afraid. . . .
'Who are you? What is your game?' . . . Just as now you're
looking at me—why have I brought Doctor Arnold here? Yes,
you are wondering."

"I never thought of such a thing," Connie answered in astonishment. "It was very good of you. Gus and I know so little about
doctors. We wouldn't have known what to do without you."

Laurie colored.

"You needn't be polite. I know the whole town talks about
it. They knew as soon as Doctor Arnold came to town that summer seven years ago. It was all my fault—I knew I was acting
like a fool. I knew they said I ran after him—they still say it, you
needn't bother to smooth things over. Well, what of it? I never
was brazen about anything in my life before—but you have to
be about the things you want. Can't expect people to just hand
them over. And this mattered too much to me. I'd have run all
over the world crying for him. Wouldn't care who saw."

"I didn't know about it," Connie said weakly. She didn't want to hear more. It hurt her to see naked feelings. She recoiled from them as she would from an indecent picture, frightened, a little sick, as a too civilized tourist might look on a primitive dance.

"But he won't let me now," Laurie whispered fiercely. "And so far as that goes there's nothing between us now. Do you know what he says? That I'm the type who runs after orchestra leaders, gets crushes on the riding-teacher or the captain of the steamer—that that's all I feel for him. . . . All right. Does it make it less real—less painful?"

She turned to the window as Gus and the doctor came back in the room. The doctor did not look at her but picked up his hat quickly and took Connie's hand.

"You'll be getting along," he said. "A few things to be settled first—that's all—whether Dell River's the place for you—"

Go some place without Decker?

"I couldn't leave Dell River," said Connie and shook her head decisively.

"I see," answered the doctor amiably. "Well, Laurie?"

"Tell her she's got to be careful, tell her she mustn't talk or sing," Gus begged the doctor.

"I'll be very good," Connie answered them both. She was no longer annoyed at Gus treating her like a child. It was dear old Gus who was the child. She and the doctor understood. Gus and Laurie were the children. She watched the two callers scurry out to the car, their outlines blurred in the slanting rain. Gus sat on the chair, gloomily watching her, trying to find proof in her face somehow of the doctor's diagnosis.

"If you should have to go away—"

"We haven't the money, Gus. Even if I would consent to go. Where does he suggest? The South? Doctors are always suggesting the South."

"No," said Gus heavily. "A sanitarium in the Southwest, he says."

Connie frowned.

"Oh, no," she said. "They can't take me there. Oh, no."

Then her momentary fear vanished again in the consoling reflection that here was something amusing to tell Decker when he came. "Great specialists must have their great names for the simplest diseases. Even laziness has a name and a most imposing treatment." She wondered how soon he would come. She wanted to talk to someone civilized to break the trouble-some memory of Laurie's shocking bluntness and the doctor's brutal eyes. The raindrops on the window trembled, swelled into eyes, dripped tears, and were whipped off by other rain-drops that in turn, swelled into eyes. Doctor Arnold's.

Connie shivered.

꒳

Laurie, driving the doctor to the Benjamin home on his weekly Dell River visit, was hard-eyed and defiant.

"Let them talk," she said to Miss Manning. "It can't make them like me less. If gossip makes them think about me, so much the better. At least they know I exist."

But Dell River knew little and cared less about Laurie's connection with the doctor. He was one of those smooth-acting city men often seen about the old Neville home in summer, people Laurie picked up probably on her travels and occasion-ally introduced at some Dell River gathering to make the natives feel uncomfortably crude. In their indifferent polite-ness Laurie thought she read suspicion, even certainty. They saw, perhaps, that when she first fastened her violent adoration on this man she did not dream of a wife back in Baltimore, and they laughed, perhaps, at such naïveté in the Neville girl for all her fancy education. They suspected—oh, Laurie was sure they did!—her hysterical insistence on an affair, they probably saw how angrily he tried to retreat and finally the furtive des-perate moments in his office, on lonely roads between Dell

River and his hospital. They knew of his final breaking off
with her because of his perfectly stupid complacent little wife
and they must have said, "See how little money and French
schools can get a woman, even a handsome one, in our little
closed respectable community. Her money could help a doctor's career but instead he chooses a dumb little plain
wife—not through love but through pure respectability." They
must see now how eagerly she pounced upon any professional
excuse to see him again, how wretched it made her to know he
was still attracted by her but was stronger than steel against
her. She sensed—and so the town must, too—she thought—
how quickly some appeal from her could change him into ice
and she knew—if she could adopt this controlled ease herself
he might come back to her. Yet this knowledge never helped
her to control her hysteria, she saw herself at each meeting
ruining each shred of hope by eagerness. Now that Mrs.
Benjamin's illness was an excuse to bring him often to Dell
River she was constantly in a state of tension, and Miss
Manning's power to still her nerves was diminished. The little
routine of her days since her parents' death several years
before—the little duties invented to make believe life was not
so futile as it seemed were rushed through carelessly as the silly
time-markers they were. Letters to girls she'd gone to school
with—

>"My dear Elizabeth—
>I have not heard from you for months but Bella
>writes your trip to India was a heavenly experience. I
>wish you would write me about it—Manny and I
>might go over next year . . ."
>"My dear Eleanor—
>So sorry not to get to the Foxdale luncheon when I
>was East and see all the girls but I was shopping
>and—"

It wasn't that these old school-friends, now busy matrons and not as anxious to correspond as Laurie was, were so dear to her—indeed she'd almost forgotten how they looked—but letters were all she had to look forward to from day to day. They came on the morning breakfast tray, were slowly read and discussed with Manny and then put away to be taken out after dinner as they sat before the fire with their coffee and cigarettes and so little to talk about! . . . Now such answers as came were wasted for Laurie paced up and down the rooms, flushed and nervous, ready to scream if Manny even attempted to distract her.

"It's no use, Manny," she exclaimed. "When a person has just one thing to think about she's got to think until her brain wears out, that's all."

The only thing that helped Manny's final surrender to the one subject was her theories as to how all this misery could have been avoided.

"The advantages my parents gave me—that's at the bottom of everything!" Laurie said savagely. "Bringing me up to be different from the people I was to live with—so that they hate me—"

"They don't!"

"—and despise me and I'm afraid of them. So I'm afraid of everyone. Only with him I feel strong. Sometimes with you—but always with him—"

But no one in Dell River knew the things Laurie thought they suspected. They didn't care. Even Connie Benjamin finally decided that the reason Laurie had interested herself in her illness was someway related to Blaine Decker—perhaps Laurie was in love with him, and therefore concerned about his friends.

༄

A dreadful summer, Decker thought, each day to be balanced on the nose cautiously to keep from spilling its incipient disasters

in all directions. In the thick sultriness of Middlewestern
August it took godlike energy to preserve the pleasant insanity
necessary to happiness. No breeze stirred the blue curtains of
his apartment by night and by day the sun beat down with savage diligence. Decker would be in bed feeling the night's
humidity modulate in the dry morning heat and he would
think, "Today I must work—practice the Sonata, plan a new
course for—say a history of music or a study of instruments—
talk it over with Marshall—send for books. At least if I must
teach I might show how much better I can do it than the average school teacher. I could do that."

But the plan for a new course usually ended in being discussed—as a cast-off idea—with Connie later in the day. A
brilliant plan and—"So like you," Connie admiringly observed,
"giving yourself away completely to students who don't half
appreciate what you've given up for them." The fact that these
plans went no further did not detract from Decker's courage in
Connie's eyes but these unfinished ideas, discarded the day
they appeared, worried Decker as a sign of approaching age
and resignation. When he finally got out of bed in the morning
he pattered about the place in frayed dressing-gown and slip-
pers for hours making coffee and toast, tidying up, making
tasks to delay the actual work of the day. He sat at the desk
giving up all idea of a cool breeze at either window, and with
different colored inks played at his old game of arranging concert programs. No Debussy if there was Brahms, was his
theory of programs, and no little group of French moderns if
he began with Bach. Years ago he had played this game
according to rules—no number he couldn't play well, but now
he was lazy, listing pieces he had only heard about in newspapers. When he sat down to the piano it was usually to play the
opening bars of some old favorite then to stop dead as his
memory collapsed, too upset by this failure to look up the piece
in his cabinet. His fingers were stiff, they moved woodenly
about the keys, strangers to music, and Decker, after the first

bungled chords, was too angry to practice. The only consolations were the little songs such as Miss Manning sang, and he would dwell tenderly on these simple accompaniments and sometimes take the books over to Connie's to play in the afternoon. "This was probably one of your favorites," he would say and play a little bergerette. Connie, who might never have known of the song's existence till that moment, would smile sentimentally and murmur, "I'm not sure I could do it now. It suited my voice once but now—"

"Too light for operatic shadings," Decker would say understandingly. "You're quite right. But it is charming—let me play it for you again."

As Connie grew better they sometimes went on leisurely walks across the river into the fields and sometimes Mimi would follow them later with a picnic basket. They sat in the clearing in the woods where Connie had once sung to the May morning, and they talked of music until the careers they once planned were the careers they actually had had but had given up for the superior joys of simple living. Mimi sat, cross-legged, on the grass, eating sandwiches, her round eyes moving respectfully from Decker to her mother, and as Decker's voice grew more and more British and her mother's more silvery in their mutual appreciations Mimi would blush, thinking of Helen's mockery of these very affectations. When her mother would sigh, "At least it's something to know one could have had fame—we should be grateful for that, for so many people never have even that assurance"—Mimi would try not to remember Helen's caustic remarks, "Listen, nobody has to give up anything unless they really want to or are too darned weak. If Mama really could have done anything she would have—if anybody wants something all she needs do is go and get it. There aren't any excuses."

Decker ignored Mimi and Helen though he managed a smile of fixed politeness when they interrupted his discussions or when their mother called upon them to perform some errand. He disliked young girls just as he did household pets, they were always upsetting things or brushing against you, ruining a well-turned phrase with some unfortunate interruption. In school he saw them without prejudice in groups but too often one of these girls would stop at his desk to ask questions. If they concerned music or were inquiries into future professional work Decker forgot they were silly little girls and expounded on foreign and domestic teachers, on the Thorners and Witherspoons and on teachers long dead or settled definitely in Berlin; he loved explaining the differences in their various methods, this one had a tendency to overstrain the upper register, this one pushed the student too fast into public engagements—he went over all the musical patter of his first student years, enriched it with anecdotes about a certain director in Milan, an impresario in Munich, and allowed a hint to enter here and there of his own former advantageous connections. Meantime the girl, who had only wanted to study with some good cheap teacher in Pittsburgh or Columbus so that she might some day teach privately in Dell River or sing solos in the church, would squirm uneasily and grow so appalled at the magnificent picture Decker was evoking that she could only murmur a faint, "Oh, thank you—thank you"—and scurry away, thoroughly disheartened.

Boys were not so bad for they were, underneath their rudeness, sensitive and mentally alert, so the music teacher felt, whereas girls were callous and futile, designed only to weaken the male. Decker thought very little about his students individually unless as happened sometimes one betrayed an unusual intelligence about music. He had overcome to some degree his early terror of sheer youth, though he still could not face the main auditorium on a crowded Friday morning without a shudder of pure distaste for such uncontrolled energy as was here massed, the air always seemed charged with the dangerous electricity of youth, any moment a volt might strike you. But he enjoyed the effects of their mingled voices and in so far as these young people represented instruments of sound he almost loved them.

The Benjamin girls were tolerable only because of their mother and once in a while he studied them with detached curiosity to find points of resemblance. Mimi's eyes for instance—and Helen's profile. There were times when he was distinctly annoyed at their mother's fugitive bursts of interest in them, but this was not jealousy so much as surprise that so intelligent a woman as Constance could find any fascination in the hopeless gropings of youth. Unless they were actively jumping about or noisy, they did not bother him, but the occasional proofs of their existence—a squeal from Mimi over a nest of field-mice or a snake if they were outdoors—made him impatient. Connie, even in their finest discussions, did not mind having the children about since she had learned long ago to shut her ears to whatever might not harmonize with her private thoughts.

In many ways Connie's illness had been an advantage to both of them for she was reading more. Laurie Neville had ordered different musical monthlies sent to her and now both Connie and Decker pored over them from cover to cover, discussed even the advertising and constantly exclaimed over some concert they would love to hear or some modern song they would most certainly—if Connie's health had only been better—have tried out. Before her sickness they had felt that they knew by instinct everything to be known about music and everything that was going on. If at Laurie Neville's someone had mentioned a new artist's sensational debut in the East, Decker would have said patronizingly, "Oh yes, of course—but he's very likely just a flash in the pan—" for to betray curiosity would be a confession of his isolation from the cosmopolitan world, as he always assumed both to himself and others that he caught all these little rumors and many artists' secrets in the ordinary course of his professional life. He was by no means, he tacitly assured them, cut off from the centers of culture just because he taught in Dell River. Ah no, indeed.

As for Connie she had ruled her life on the same principle of being instinctively in touch with music without being forced to study any current chronicles. Now that sickness excused her from any pretense of practising she began to talk to Decker of private recitals she might have given—now alas, impossible!— in Dell River and eagerly Decker mapped out programs she should have given. Miss Neville would gladly have given her an afternoon at her home; he, of course, would have accompanied her, playing an opening number himself—say the Waldstein Sonata. He had not played it for years but if Fate had not so cruelly intervened once more, he would certainly have played it at her recital. They began to look at other singers' programs listed in *Musical America* and they would smile sadly at each other as if—"The very things we would have done! The very same things!" It really seemed that these plans for a series of recitals not only in Dell River but in Greentown and surrounding towns, had been on the very verge of completion when the illness had ruined all.

"It almost seems," mused Connie, "as if there were some definite god working against us—"

"It does indeed," agreed Decker in a low grave voice and both were silent and humble over the gifts which had so excited the fear and envy of the gods.

"It must mean we would never have been happy if we'd won out," pursued Connie.

"Exactly," said Decker solemnly. "Success would have destroyed us."

⁂

As school days once more approached Decker grew irritable and confused as a banker might who has lost, through his own carelessness, a fortune and with only himself to blame must hurl recriminations at the whole world. In such a way the summer was lost, he had not practiced, he had not planned new courses, he had not taken soul-refreshing weekends at the lake, he had not read, but drowsing through the hot days he had used over and over the same old thoughts; he had, for Mrs. Benjamin, turned his mind inside out and upside down, evoked and embellished memories of his past until they were thin with repetition, he had examined each microscopic detail of his past, selecting bits for Connie's afternoon as the Papa Robin might choose bits for his nest. The days, pointed toward those afternoon hours together, had seemed to some purpose but with the school year close before him and time laid out in terms of accomplishment, these vacation months seemed to have been waste, sheer waste.

Decker liked to think of himself as someone, unlike the provincials with whom his life was cast, who was constantly at the spring of things, living a rich, full sort of life. But September always loomed bluntly before him saying, "Well, here you are, at the same place you were last year, sentenced for another year."

Through the bars of September he saw the monotony of another year, the definite death of the improbable hopes always lurking in his mind. Despairingly he saw the great drastic moves he should have made in June to free himself. How wastefully he had allowed the days to slip past, raising no hand to stop the certain prison they were building for him! He might have written to New York bureaus—of course concerts were out of the question for him now but at least he would be in touch with the main offices and be able to say to Marshall or anyone else, "I've just had a letter from Hartzell and Tones— they manage most of the big artists, you know." . . . It wouldn't matter what they said, the point would be that something might be stirring, something might happen to leave a gate open in that September prison.

Louisa Murrell, even, seemed to have had a most amazingly rich summer, merely because she'd spent a week or two at the Neville shore cottage with a room of her own and candles on the table at dinner. She fluttered in and out of The Oaks with such an important air that the rumor got abroad she was engaged to be married. And Marshall! His ten-day trip around the national capital had given him the assurance that a season or two in Legislature might have given better men. He came back with a greater sense of the dignity of his own position, and one of his first deeds on arriving in Dell River was to send for Decker to discuss improvements in his department.

They sat in the glass-enclosed porch of the Marshall home, a rather staid Victorian house painted a dull pink by a light-minded tenant and left nakedly in a great stretch of lawn with not one tree to hide its shame.

"What Mrs. Marshall and I planned," said Marshall, offering Decker a cigar, then leaning back in a gaudily cretonned chair, "was a sort of historical pageant on Thanksgiving with all the old camp songs, don't you know? That's the idea this trip gave us around Mt. Vernon and up the Potomac."

"I should imagine it would," said Decker with polite sarcasm.

"It was really Mrs. Marshall's idea," admitted Marshall with not a little pride and a jerk of the thumb toward the interior where the noise of a carpet sweeper could be heard. "She has a lot of ideas that way."

"Indeed!" Decker commented and then said with a sweep of his hand. "Of course if that's the sort of thing you want I can take charge of it very easily. True, it's often been done and I like to think we have a little more originality here in Dell River but then the conventional thing is simpler—of course."

Slightly stung by Decker's lack of admiration, Marshall puffed silently at his cigar.

"I think we should have examinations in general music," he said. "I talked to some other teachers at the hotel in Washington. And I think you're too lax with rehearsal cutting—lots of those boys never show up except for the Friday roll call."

Decker, who had often suspected this but was too preoccupied with the difficulties of teaching to go in for individual discipline, grew very frigid at this accusation.

"I think you exaggerate, Professor Marshall," he said stiffly. "I believe I can handle my rehearsals as well as an outside observer."

"Hardly an outside observer, Decker," said Marshall, irritated. "Anyway there are a great many changes I'd like to suggest in the music department. Say a history course in music, for instance."

"Impossible," said Decker as if he had not in his more active moments planned just such a course. "The school isn't ready for it. The casual way we'd have to teach it would not be worthwhile. No, Marshall, I'm distinctly opposed to these so-called popular courses in serious subjects."

"Well, of course, if you're too busy," said Marshall, a little alarmed lest his talk should lead Decker to feel too much the importance of his department. "Mrs. Marshall talked to the teachers and got the idea—a lot more in fact."

Decker was still ruffled by the implied criticism of the way he conducted his department.

"I think I explained to you when I took this position," he said, "that I had very carefully laid out my plans for the next three years. I felt that I made that quite clear. Not that I don't appreciate Mrs. Marshall's suggestion. It must be splendid to feel you have such a clever little wife."

"Oh, Mrs. Marshall herself used to teach, you know—she had the English classes," Marshall grew more amiable. "Nothing like having cooperation right in your home. Frankly, Decker, I got along twice as fast after I married. I don't suppose I'd ever have been anything but a history and chemistry teacher if I hadn't met Mrs. Marshall."

"Amazing!" said Decker, not at all interested in the romance of his superior.

"That's why I'd hoped you'd get married—maybe this summer," Marshall continued confidentially. "You'd be a much

better teacher, Decker. Mrs. Marshall and I figured out that that
was what was the matter with you. You need a wife. You'd
have more ambition then. Take more interest."

Decker felt as if Marshall had genially placed a large boot
right on his solar plexus. He was outraged at this insulting
suggestion of marriage, and that such inferior people as the
Marshalls should feel it their privilege to weigh his situation
and prescribe. As if his case were a "problem" instead of
cause for envy and admiration! He could not speak for indignation.

"Yes, you'd find yourself a lot more adaptable if you married," pursued Marshall, mistaking his silence for docility. "And
there's no getting around it, a man as close to forty as you are
ought to be settled. It's all very well living alone but nothing
like a few woman's touches around a place."

Decker's stomach did a rapid contraction, something like a
somersault as the kaleidoscopic picture of what having a wife
involved sped across his brain—corsets on the piano, nail files
and combings all over the place, awful women's magazines
mixed up with his music and in his bed a soft, pliant creature—
merely imagining the obscene softness of the female skin gave
him gooseflesh—the hint of intimacy with this mythical wife
made him shudder with horror and revolt. He glared at
Marshall wishing there were some easy annihilation for such
busybodies.

"Have you seen Louisa since she's gotten back?" asked
Marshall slyly but the connection was lost on Decker.

"I don't think so," he answered stupidly.

"Looking splendid!" said Marshall, the matchmaker,
heartily, but now a little afraid if he pushed the matter too far
he'd have to get a new music teacher in the middle of the term.
"Did you have a good summer?"

Decker shook off his momentary nausea and rose to go.

"Simply delightful!" he announced. "Long walks through
this gorgeous country—I assure you it's much nicer than

Brittany!—and occasional runs up to the Shore, some business meetings with a chap from the East who wants me to accompany artists again, but of course I'm much too contented here—and then working constantly at my piano! An ideal summer, thank you!"

"I suppose Dell River isn't as bad as some places in summer—especially if you can't get away," said Marshall sympathetically. Decker twirled his hat.

"When you've travelled as much as I have, my dear fellow," he said with smiling superiority, "you will realize how rare a charming spot like Dell River is, and nothing could persuade you to leave it for any of the usual tours. Well, I must be off!"

And he swung gallantly down the cinder path to the street.

Marshall stared after him, his mouth still slightly agape, not sure just where he had been wounded but certain that he disliked his music-teacher with an undignified intensity.

∽

Laurie Neville's doctor was helping Connie but Gus hung around the house gloomily each time he called, often interrupting the light chatter of his wife with, "Don't let her talk so much, Doctor. She makes herself worse that way."

Lately he would bring up the subject of the doctor's fees too, insisting that this was none of Miss Neville's affair and he would not allow anyone to help him with his family troubles. Connie was more indignant at this humiliating candor than she had ever been before, and could find no words to ease the awkward situation Gus invited. It took longer and longer each time to restore her old reassuring thought, "Gus is so true and simple! He only acts that way because he cares so deeply. And after all he's been so good to me in his kind natural way. No one else in the world would ever have been so kind."

Once she took him to task for dickering over the bill the minute the doctor entered the house.

"Well, by God, I can't go on paying it forever," Gus finally shouted angrily. "More money for six months of doctoring than I make in a year."

"But it's almost over," said Connie, surprised that the actual financial worry was at the bottom of Gus' frankness more than bad manners or concern over her own condition. "Remember we've been well for years—most people have doctor bills every year."

"Almost over!" exclaimed Gus. He shook his finger at her. "Do you know what that man says? That you'll never get well. It's going to be this way and maybe worse from now on. All he can do is to keep you from getting worse! The best food—no work—no worry! That costs money! I've got a right to ask him where we stand!"

Connie looked blankly at him. To herself and Decker she had referred to her disease as her "breakdown" as if it were the result of acute intellectual labors and a fine nervous maladjustment. She had succeeded in ignoring the doctor's hints, invariably adopting the tone that his calls were more social than professional, and gliding as quickly as possible over the ruder details of his visits. The few times actual pain had forced her to face reality she had been in such terror of death that she was glad to banish both truth and fear when the pain left her. Of course she would not die and of course these little disorders were not to be worried over. But Gus' bluntness frightened her.

"You mean I won't ever be able to take care of the house— to play the piano—to sing —"

Gus was shamed by her trembling voice.

"Well, he says you mustn't tire yourself. The girls can do the work anyway. Mimi can cook and Helen can work when she's a mind to."

"Yes, the girls are good," Connie said in the queer strained voice of someone in a dream. "But what about the money for the treatments and all the things he says I must have? We haven't much."

Gus looked down at his thick-soled boots.

"We can manage."

"But how—Gus, tell me...."

He raised his eyes.

"We've got the shop," he said. "I guess we could make out in those three rooms upstairs. That way I can look after you more when the girls are in school."

Live over the shop? She looked at him blankly.

"Decker'll find a place," Gus said gruffly. "It's the only thing to do as long as this goes on."

"But what about this house" Connie asked limply. "We've always lived here."

"Sell it," Gus said. He got up and came over to her chair, patted her on the head. "We've got to have the money to get you well, you know. I don't say we'll have to move but we always can. You just wondered how we'd manage the bills and— well—I had to tell you. So there you are."

"Yes," said Connie. "I see."

She went to bed, keeping the danger and confusion away from her mind; her head was empty and dull. For the first time the effort to keep out fear kept out Decker as well.

꓿

Gus said no more about financial worry and Connie dismissed it from her thoughts. The doctor came less often for her improvement depended not so much on his treatment as the daily precautions against excitement. Laurie Neville and her companion continued from their shore house to New York for their annual fortnight of shopping and theater-going and Louisa Murrell could not resist showing the note Laurie wrote her from New York as against the picture postcards she sent to the other teachers at The Oaks. The old Sunday teas at Mrs. Benjamin's were resumed with Louisa preparing the supper assisted by the girls and sometimes by Decker, which gave the parties a gay bohemian touch offsetting the dampening effect of Connie's illness. After tea the little new victrola was placed on the library table and Decker fussed over it as jealously as if only years of training could enable one to operate this very special instrument. Now, although he possessed very few records he liked to believe they were the vital ones and certainly had persuaded Connie and Louisa of this.

"Which shall it be first tonight?" he would ask after the records had been carefully dusted off, the machine adjusted to his taste. "Shall we begin with the Pathétique or save it for the last?"

Connie, lying back in her chair, would see that his fingers were on the Fifth Symphony so she would say. "Let's begin with the Fifth—I'm not in a Russian mood just yet."

And Decker would play the Beethoven as if he had not planned to do that first no matter what was said. Connie closed her eyes, each record might have had cut into it the separate dream it sent Connie. On the Beethoven she thought of Tony and transformed their love by this pure music into a Lancelot-Elaine legend and slowly it grew into the fable that Gus had appeared not so much as her savior but as Duty, a worthy figure for whom she had renounced the too ecstatic pleasures of ideal love. In the Tchaikovsky record were the invisible grooves where the dream story of her triumphant career unwound and so each piece became known to her only by the definite images it evoked. Gus stayed in the kitchen or went up to bed during these concerts but he kept the bedroom door open for the music soothed him the same way the barber's beer did, gratifying his stomach in the same rich way. Sometimes his voice would be heard as he leaned out the front window to hail his daughter. "Helen! Where are you going?"

"I'm only going for a walk," was the sullen response.

"Who's that with you?"

"Just Hank."

"Well, see that you get back here before dark."

These clearly heard exchanges did not interrupt the pleasure of the three downstairs, least of all Connie who usually smiled gently as if the impulsiveness of youth was charming to observe. Louisa tried to give an answering smile but hers was often rather strained since Helen's independence was regarded with more alarm in the school than it was at home. But one couldn't very well speak of a daughter's misdemeanors to a mother, dewey-eyed over Beethoven, even if one was—as Louisa definitely was not—that sort of helpful friend. The nearest she could get to the subject of Helen was to speak, from time to time, of the troublesome case of Honey Busch, who had taken to running away from home every few days and was brought home by officers when Busch himself couldn't find her.

"That must be so hard on poor Mrs. Busch," said Connie.

"Oh, no," said Louisa. "She chuckles over it. She says, 'Isn't that Honey of mine a card? And don't the boys just run after her? They never looked at me, the boys didn't when I was a girl!' That's the way she takes it."

"Funny old Busch," mused Decker and he and Connie nodded their heads fondly.

Decker sat up late nights with catalogs, checking the records he would buy if he had the money, and stayed in the school office on Saturdays to type in neat classifications the list of this prospective collection. The pages were then placed in a leather notebook, its title page inscribed—"Blaine Decker Collection." He spent as much time weighing the eligibility of each piece as if he were actually putting out money for it and many times, after judicial consultation with Connie, decided that such and such a piece was too light to be included in a permanent collection. When Laurie sent him some foreign catalogs he was enchanted though—as he explained to Connie—these imports were likely to ruin him!

Louisa was pleased with this new interest for she had more spending money than her two friends and could often, after listening to a discussion about some piece, appear later in the

Benjamin parlor with the coveted record under her arm, her
face beaming with pleasure at being able to provide such a surprise. Louisa had a new source of strength in her summer's
fortnight at Miss Neville's. At The Oaks she could put down
any insult from Swasey or Emmons with a casual reference to
her gay evenings at the shore, all the charming little ways Laurie
had shown respect for her opinions. If Swasey laughed at the
diary Louisa was keeping in verse Louisa had only to say,
"Goodness, Laurie and Miss Manning were so embarrassing the
way they insisted on showing my diary to the friends from
Chicago who drove down—that newspaper editor you know,
and that University of Wisconsin professor. They seemed to
think it ought to be published as a sort of calendar. Goodness
knows I try not to be too personal in case it *should* be published."

Louisa knew this vantage ground could last only as long as
some mystery surrounded the two weeks and daily new facts
were grudgingly put out so that in due time every little incident
would be known to The Oaks, no dark horses of suitors, or
unreported conversations with Laurie could be mentioned for
The Oaks would know all. She could put down Swasey's impu-
dent references to "the Professor" as they called Decker by
saying, "Laurie says he's easily the most interesting man we've
had stay in Dell River." One evening the two other teachers got
the upper hand. They were sitting in The Oaks' dreary living-
room, the table under the forlorn light of the green chandelier
littered with papers to be graded, a plate of apples and a slim box
of chocolate peppermints. Miss Emmons occasionally smoked a
cigarette but it kept her awake and always gave her a headache
so she forgot it when unobserved. Louisa had turned from one
theme paper to the next until the mere sight of the day's title, "A
Day in the Country," gave her a chill, so the papers lay idly in
her lap while she stared at the bright blue gas logs in the grate.

"Thinking of your sweetie?" teased Miss Emmons. "Look
at her, Swasey, you can always tell by that dreamy look who
she's got on her mind."

"Which is it he likes best—you or Mrs. Benjamin?" asked Miss Swasey. "He's more of a ladies' man than I ever gave him credit for being."

Louisa drew her mouth into a line of disgust.

"You people don't understand the simplest things," she said coldly. "You don't even know there's such a thing as intellectual companionship, that's much more important than a silly love affair."

"I'll bet he's in love with the Benjamin woman," speculated Swasey. "I think they're just using you as a blind, Louisa. If I were you I wouldn't stand for it."

Louisa was exasperated.

"Oh, can't you see they're friends because they're the only two people in Dell River who could have been something else? She could have been a great singer—you've heard all about that—and you know that he started out studying to be a concert pianist. They can talk over music and careers and no one else in Dell River—except myself—knows what they gave up.

Miss Emmons decided to light a cigarette to give more distinction to her own speech.

"I didn't ask them to give up anything," she said lightly. "My theory is that if a person has the stuff he can deliver it—he doesn't let anything else come first."

"He certainly isn't modest about his talent," agreed Miss Swasey. "Every time he opens his mouth he lets you know how good he is."

"Why shouldn't he?" blazed Louisa, the most modest of women. "What's so fine about modesty—except for it making other people feel superior? A person can afford to be modest after he's got everything he wants. When everybody knows you're good you don't need to brag. It's like generosity—it's easy to be generous after you've had plenty—but it's no credit to you. Modesty's no credit to anyone—it's just a social grace."

"Well, well!" ejaculated Miss Emmons, wide-eyed. "I hadn't asked for that. Is 'Modesty' your class subject for tomorrow?"

"Come down to earth, Louisa," advised Miss Swasey. "You know if Blaine Decker or Mrs. Benjamin were really good they wouldn't be here in Dell River just talking."

"How can you be sure what anyone would do or be under other circumstances?" Louisa angrily retorted. Her papers had slid to the floor, the corrected mixed with the uncorrected, and her face was flushed with unaccustomed indignation. "When someone doesn't accomplish what he set out to do it doesn't mean he hasn't enough talent. Maybe he hasn't the character, maybe he's too fine to cut people's throats and step on them the way you have to do to get on the map."

"You can't expect me to believe in such a person until I've seen him at least make a try at what he claims to do so well," defended Miss Emmons mildly.

"You might believe in his ideals," sputtered Louisa. "All I'm saying is that a man might be too fine for success—instead of not being good enough he might be too good. That's all I mean."

Sulkily she picked up the papers. Miss Emmons shrugged her shoulders and passed the peppermints to Miss Swasey. They exchanged a look. Louisa stared fixedly at "A Day in the Country" trying to get calm enough—as she never could in speaking of Decker or Mrs. Benjamin—to make some telling dispassionate remark that would completely crush her audience, something to the effect that it took more than average intelligence to recognize genius when it passed, anyway. But the amused silence of the other two women made her suspect that anything she said would only entertain them.

"All the same," said Miss Emmons in a low voice, "there's more than intellectual companionship between Decker and the Benjamin woman, and I'm only surprised more people haven't noticed it."

"Not really!" exclaimed Miss Swasey, highly pleased.

Louisa sat very still with her mouth in a prim tight line. She was so angry at the two women that it was all she could do to

compose her mind later on for her nightly poem in her diary—
eight lines this time on "A Woodland Path."

જ

Early spring found the Benjamins installed over the shoe-shop.
Mimi was enchanted with the little flat. Its tiny kitchen, the
porch where her mother sometimes slept, the sound of victrolas
and pianos being tried out in the Music Store nearby were all
advantages not obtainable in the ordinary home. Since Helen
disliked housework and her mother was not equal to it, the
place was practically Mimi's playhouse, and the girls in the
Domestic Science kitchen envied her this responsibility. Helen
herself was pleased over the excuse now provided her for being
constantly in touch with whatever excitement the town could
offer—certainly no one could scold her for "running the
streets" nights when she lived in the very heart of town. With
no place to entertain boyfriends she had excellent reason for late
automobile rides and constant visits to girlfriends' homes. Her
mother could not blame her for not spending an extra minute
in the home for every move she made brought forth sharp
rebukes from her father. She could not run down the steps to
slip out without Gus calling from the shop, "Helen! Why must
you paint your face so to go to the butcher shop? You, not sixteen yet!"

"I'm past sixteen!" Helen would retort.

"Wipe that red off your lips! Pull your skirts down! What's
the matter with your eyes, you look like a damn movie girl!
Let's see what it is you've done to yourself. What've you done to
your eyebrows, hey? What's that stuff on your eyes, hey? Go
right back upstairs and make yourself look like a decent girl."

With such constant heckling it was surely no wonder Helen
was in a perpetual sulk, venting her righteous wrath on Mimi
when her father was out of hearing and allowing her gloomy
face to indicate prodigious dissatisfaction to her mother. Connie

refused to let Helen's discontent affect her, for it was hard enough as it was to get accustomed to the change in their lives. If the past few weeks of trips to Doctor Arnold's hospital for fluoroscoping, X-rays, serum injections of one sort and another—if all these expenses had made it wiser to sell the house to the first bidder and take over the shop's upstairs then hers was too serious a condition to bear much scrutiny. She was crushed with fear but the doctor found her really improving after the move and of course it was logical that the nearness of Gus made it possible to do without a nurse.

Decker had moved to The Oaks where Louisa, in secret triumph, saw this male intrusion change Swasey's and Emmons' cynicism into fawning respect for his every mood. Decker dared not tell Connie how uncomfortable his new quarters made him lest she reproach herself for her inconsiderate illness, but he hated the feeling of being in the "teachers' house" as if he were no longer Decker, the individual, the man about town who did a few hours' lecturing in the schools, but the drab, doomed schoolmaster. The Oaks' living room with its table piled high each evening with school papers, textbooks, educational magazines, made his heart sink, though for the three women the room had now become almost wickedly gay with music notebooks shining amid Latin papers and English themes, as significantly masculine as the soft fedora hung on the hall-tree among the women's wraps. Miss Emmons no longer sat down to the old upright piano after supper to fumble through last year's song hit, or inspired by Sunday dinner try to struggle through "The Rosary" to Miss Swasey's falsetto obbligato. No, the piano was turned over to the maestro, copies of "St. Louis Blues" and "I'm Sorry, Dear" were hastily concealed in Miss Emmons' bottom drawer and the piano rack left free for a more musicianly display.

Decker was made uncomfortable by this expectancy. If he wanted to play when the room was empty he heard their footsteps tiptoeing respectfully past the door and his fingers made ridiculous mistakes. If, at dinner, he referred lightly to this or that prelude he was bound to be requested to play it later on and it irritated him that he must so abruptly face the results of his words, that he must privately acknowledge that this piece, once so familiar to him, was more than he could even attempt now. So, for weeks the silent piano held proudly on its rack a worn Beethoven collection and opened out over this, as if constantly practised, a frayed "Fantasie Stücke."

Louisa had a quiet revenge in seeing the deference paid to Professor Decker by his detractors. She was cynically amused when Decker's table talk of his friend Starr Donnell, the novelist, sent both teachers to the little library with requests for Donnell's works, and stories about Ilsa Darmster, that strange, exotic woman, kept the Misses Swasey and Emmons in a whispered argument upstairs lasting half the night on just what Ilsa's fascination had been and if Professor Decker hadn't been a little more involved with her—oh naughty, sophisticated man!—than he cared to reveal.

Louisa visited Connie often and on the latter's good days they walked together around the Square or sat down on a bench near the fountain. For Connie after a while the little flat had a compelling charm merely by its association with Decker. She found a certain satisfaction in living behind walls that had known his shadow, that had shielded his secret thoughts. Sometimes this new intimacy made her feel shy with him, afraid that her face should reveal some guilty admission. There were days when her thoughts of Decker in a hundred different aspects whirled in her head like a color wheel, her heart raced, the fever carried her to a pitch approaching ecstasy. There was the familiar sense of something audaciously wondrous about to happen, then, as these premonitions of joy proved unfulfilled, symptoms of physical weakness rather than of psychic power, a weight of sickening fatigue would drop upon her, it seemed to her that to weep or to smile was labor beyond her strength. The next day, however, the same anticipation would mount once

more, images of Decker would speed through her brain and
after a while she no longer tried to keep them within the
bounds of reason but allowed and even watched with tired
curiosity the distortions of face and deed.

As spring grew she thought of the rosebush by the porch
and the bleeding hearts by the hedge. She missed the fresh
smell of wet, tumbled earth and lilacs—her garden in May.
Louisa brought her a canary and this she hung in the front window over a box of geraniums, conjuring an imaginary forest of
birds from its fluttering solo. Through the rainbow window at
the back of the apartment she could look across the court to the
fields surrounding the church and school. This picture varied
magically according to the glass and Connie used to grow
absorbed in these changes like a child with a stereopticon,
watching the fairy-tale brilliance of Dell River change to
ghostly chill through blue glass and to a candy heaven through
crimson. This pastime held her more and more after Decker
told her the village under ruby glass seemed to him a stage
Valhalla, so that, added to her own pleasure was the conjectur-
ing as to how this would appear through Decker's eyes.

Louisa too, was amused to compare the shifting moods
induced by the rainbow panes. It seemed to her that Decker
and Connie were a little like these tinted panes, and she did not
want to look at life except as transformed through their colored
light. It was the same way with love—a dreary—often ridiculous business when studied realistically but what a heavenly
luster it had when viewed through her poets!

Louisa was almost able to see Helen with Mrs. Benjamin's
eyes, who sighed sentimentally, "Ah, youth, youth!" when
Helen banged all the doors shut or refused to speak because
Papa forced her to spend an evening at home. Secretly Louisa
was terrified of Helen, she felt tired and used up merely seeing
Helen's fine hard body swinging vigorously through the school
halls as if the will and even the mind behind that physique were
sharp and splendidly cruel, unsoftened by innocence. When

there were examinations Louisa was afraid to flunk Helen, she could not stand up to the storm of righteous indignation from this pupil who had answers for every criticism. Even Mr. Marshall felt the same having once encountered her wrath. Louisa would have been frightened merely by her clean-cut ruddy beauty—she was always dashed by physical perfection in women as if no weapon in life could equal the consciousness of beauty. She envied Connie for being able to dismiss this young symbol of power with a shrug.

"What else could a mother do with a girl like Helen?" Miss Swasey wanted to know when Mrs. Benjamin's nonchalance was discussed. "She couldn't ever discipline her so she might as well pretend she sees wise old Nature working behind all those high jinks. Just what old Mrs. Busch does with Honey only of course Honey's bound to get in wrong and Helen's too shrewd for that."

One day Honey Busch came downtown wheeling a baby carriage. The rumor of this event had gone about before and Mrs. Busch had in fact hinted of it to Connie for it seemed to Honey's mother that girls would be girls and there was no difference between Helen Benjamin petting in parked autos and Honey Busch staying out all night in a barn with some farmhand. An unexpected baby now and then could only be put down to unusually high spirits and Honey's misadventure did not dismay her mother but made her child seem unusually precocious.

"She always was a caution!" she sighed to Connie with baffled pride. "Never could tell what she'd do next. . . . And the boys after her every minute. I only wished I had the beaux Honey has. That's what makes the women in this town talk about her—they're jealous. Anyway it's the prettiest baby I ever laid my two eyes on."

Honey looked pale and angelic wheeling the baby up and down slowly and looking eagerly about for people to admire it.

"Look!" she would say, plucking the sleeve of some embarrassed passer-by. "A baby!"

It was the first time she'd ever done anything unusual, and now she was proud because none of the children who teased her for not passing the third grade had babies. They still followed her up the street shouting "Crazy Honey! Crazy Honey!" but Honey was too weak and too happy to answer back, she only smiled and silently pointed to the carriage.

Connie wanted to be sympathetic but Mrs. Busch seemed to feel that Honey was only proving how normal she was after all.

"It seems funny to me," she said, "that your Helen hasn't got into trouble before but I guess she hasn't got as much life as my Honey and boys like a girl to have a little life."

The young farmhand appeared at the Busch home asking to marry Honey but Honey kept herself locked upstairs during his visit and instead of having any tender feelings for her suitor, jeered at him from her front window, calling out, "Hay foot! Hay foot!" until he whirled around at the gate to shake his fist at the unseen taunter. The sight of the sixteen-year-old Honey wheeling her baby proudly up and down the town made Dell Rivers take their daughters into grave confidence on the facts of life and fathers roared their disapproval of all beaux, springtime, and school dances.

Connie had never scolded her children beyond a gentle, "Now, now, dear!" when Helen insisted on new dresses or pocket money to go to a theater in a neighboring city. It gave her actual pain to hear Gus berating his elder daughter, though she did not object to Helen's defiant replies, certain proof, after all, that Helen was well able to handle her own wrongs. Sitting at her window she often heard their quarrels in the shop as Helen was detected coming in late or going out with her face rouged. Connie's eyes would fill with tears at Gus' harshness.

"Well, when a mother's not strong enough to handle her girls," Gus retorted, one day when she rebuked him, "the father has to take hold. We don't want her getting into Honey's fix and that's what happens when girls get their head."

Connie had no answer. Even if she had been well she would have allowed the girls to go their own way, preferring the gentle course of seeing only good in them to the disagreeable task of correction. She too had been in "trouble" as a girl, but she had not learned through that what warnings to give to daughters. She only learned that there were veils that became Truth as the stained glass window became Dell River. But even this philosophy could not be handed to one's children in a concise form. One could not say to them, "Life is a dragon certain to devour you, but if you keep your eyes shut you won't mind so much." So perhaps it was better to let Gus manage the problem in his way since she had no alternative to suggest.

Helen looked as Connie believed she herself must have looked at that age. Helen was more robust, with more color to her, but their profiles and bodies were the same. It was the resemblance that made Connie believe she knew Helen. She would not worry when Mimi reported that Helen was threatening to run away, or to go on the stage, to get married, or to quit school and sell tickets in the motion picture house.

"Helen's just talking," Connie said indulgently. "She'd never do anything to make us worry. I know my little girl."

When Blaine Decker called at his former home Helen made a point of leaving the room with a glance of silent contempt, and this unspoken criticism annoyed Decker because it could not be answered. The look seemed a complete catalog of reproaches—he was conscious of growing baldness, of shabbiness, of age, of every weakness in his armor, though Helen's frown only meant that his presence in the living room deprived her of the opportunity to entertain any of her younger friends there.

The place was unquestionably far too cramped for the family and compelled unaccustomed intimacy. Connie realized with full force what a stranger her husband was to her, and here there was no disguise or means of retreat from their lack of mutual interests. She felt helplessly cornered by the hard facts of her daily life, there was no porch or garden where she might escape. Gus' constant presence, the sight of his square, uncompromising back, even the sound of his hammering in the shop downstairs were dreary, sickening reminders of the poverty of her life; they came to stand more and more sternly between her and her own amiable world until she wept not for luxuries or conquest of fate but only for the privacy to dream of them. As her illness made her weak it made Gus strong, there was no forgetting him for a moment, and Connie felt bruised before his stiff, unyielding mind. She began to think of it not as a kind machine for grinding out wisdom but a rigid trap for platitudes. Decker grew further and further away, a storybook hero colored by the rainbow window, and the thought that Gus might come in any minute tempered the joy of their visits. It was as if Gus were allied with her illness in imprisoning her, and this quiet force could only be offset by clinging tight to Decker's hands. She needed more than spiritual understanding now, she wanted to touch him—to be sure he was as solidly near her as was Gus.

꒰

The whole town was talking about Helen Benjamin's disappearance before the news finally got to the cobbler shop. So far as the family knew she'd spent the night with the Marshall girls but Hank Herbert's confidences to his friends were soon known and Mimi, excited and frightened by turns, had to inform her parents.

"Helen told everyone in the school but me," she said. "They were married in Greentown and then they were going on to Detroit so that Hank could get a job in an automobile company, where his brother works . . . Helen told all the girls but me. . . ."

"You'll have to go after her, Gus," Connie kept repeating helplessly. She thought of Helen as that pretty little child of years ago who danced to her mother's singing; she was staggered to find that that very child could be so indifferent to family feeling. This independent gesture was a betrayal of a fond illusion, it said in essence, "See, I have my own life and you are nothing to me. I can leave without a pang, without even hinting my plans to you, for you're nothing in my life but a handicap, not even as much to me as my school chums. It's all none of your business."

But Gus was a stone wall. Helen had made her own plans, let her see them through alone. He washed his hands of her. If she wanted to make a fool of herself over that young smarty— only last week she'd declared she loathed him!—let her do it. He wouldn't raise a finger to save her. She had complained of her home, let her see how she liked the home her nineteen-year-old groom would provide.

"But we can't let her go without making some move!" Connie feebly protested.

"Why not?" asked Gus. "You did the same thing yourself. Nobody stopped you. Nobody looked for you. And you got along all right."

Connie was surprised. Gus seldom referred to her life before she met him or the circumstances of their meeting, yet now something in his tone made her suspect he had thought about it often.

"But my grandfather was different. He wasn't human, Gus! He would never have forgiven me or taken me in again. I've told you all about that."

"Maybe that's so," said Gus irritably. "I never saw your grandfather or that big home you used to tell about. All I know about you is where I found you."

In the silence that followed his words something quietly died in Connie's brain. It was the image she had built of a kind, adoring Gus, the man to whom she owed so much for all these years of quiet understanding. She looked at him with her brows knit.

"I'm only glad she's made him marry her," said Gus. He filled his pipe somberly. Connie dully watched his stained thick little hands moving about the bowl. "She won't have so much to explain to the next one that comes along. Might not have been lucky enough to find a man willing to give her a home."

"The way you did for me," Connie whispered. "Why did you do it for me, Gus? I've sometimes wondered."

"I needed a wife. I was thirty and Hans Feldt wrote me to come on here. Why not?" Gus shrugged. "I helped you—you helped me."

"But you never forgot how you found me, did you?" Connie pursued. "That's all you are sure of about me—I was just a stray to you—"

"It's all right," Gus dismissed the remark impatiently. "You've been a good wife. I got no complaint."

Connie said no more. The days and nights she had eagerly poured into his ears the stories about Manuel, about her grandfather, the Sisters . . . all the time rejoicing in his tacit sympathy . . . he had believed none of it but what he had seen with his own eyes, for the rest he shut his ears to her. She looked at him carefully, almost expecting his face to change now that his inner nature was revealing such unexpected and unfamiliar traits. A sense of having been brutally betrayed grew in her reluctantly—she'd been believing in a support that was not there, had never been there.

"Women always talk a lot. I thought there might be something in what you said," Gus said laconically. "It didn't seem likely a girl brought up with the chances you talked about would have been wandering around the country all alone, half-starved. . . . But what's the good of talking about it? You never needed to put on airs with me. I would have understood if you just told me the plain truth."

"But I did," Connie said, knowing how futile her protest was.

"Sure you did—sure," Gus soothed her. "You tell me anything you want to, that's all right. I don't hold anything against you. You're a fine girl. . . . No need to wear yourself out now talking, though."

He smoked thoughtfully for a few minutes, ready to argue about Helen if his wife spoke of the runaway again but Connie did not speak. Several times she opened her mouth as if to say something then shook her head silently. There was nothing she could say to Gus. She should have known that many years ago.

After Gus went back down to the shop Connie pressed her hands to her head as if the resulting pain would waken her mind and show her some plan of action in regard to Helen. She must scheme alone, she knew, since no help from Gus was possible. She walked up and down the little living room angry with herself for being weak, for being exhausted by even these few steps, and frightened at the unguarded thoughts that rose before her—Helen wretched and deserted as she had been once—Helen alone in a hotel room, penniless, hungry—for certainly the Herbert boy was as slim a hope as even Dell River could have provided.

"I must go to her," Connie made up her mind. "Perhaps I can't make it alone but Blaine will help me. He wouldn't fail me, no matter if Gus should."

Decker was horrified at first that she should risk the journey, but she was quietly determined. Mimi heard from the Marshall girls of the place in Greentown they were staying though there was a chance they had gone on to Detroit. Connie did not dare to tell Gus she was leaving for she was too uncertain herself how much action she could stand and knew he would not hear of her making the trip.

"But I can't let her go through all the dreadful days I did—no matter what happens," Connie told Decker.

Greentown was three hours away from Dell River on the street car. It was drizzling, the car was damp and smelled of stale pipe smoke. Decker and Connie were depressed into long silence as if this were a funeral ride and Helen a corpse rather than a bride. Connie watched the green country through the rain-stippled window and dabbed at her eyes occasionally because she felt helplessly unequal to the adventure. All very

well to try to find Helen and offer help but already her body
was trembling, the most stubborn determination could not
whip up her strength. She wished she could cling to Decker's
arm but he always drew away from her touch. As for Decker
he had given little thought to their mission, he was only concerned in supporting her, but when they arrived at the huge,
gloomy Greentown Depot he realized his position and would
gladly have turned back. Intruding on a honeymoon—asking
two of his students to return to their homes as if he were the
dean of morals, as if, indeed, he gave a continental whether
they ruined their wretched little lives or not. Only Connie's
pale resolute face kept him at her side and there was, too, an
abstract satisfaction in playing a role in a romance or scandal—
whichever it was.

It was noon when they arrived but Connie would not stop
for lunch until they had found Helen. The busy streets with
their tangle of automobiles and street cars dazed her and Decker
found the mere business of crossing the Square and hailing a
local street car a ticklish task that required all of his attention.
The address Helen had given her school-chums turned out to be
a rooming-house in the middle of town, its ground floor given
over to a grimy little millinery shop. A sign over the front-door
announced flamboyantly that this was the home of "La Belle
Hats." The elderly proprietress of the shop was the landlady as
well, for she came out when they rang the house-bell. Connie sat
down on the oak bench by the staircase. The sight of the thin old
lady with her gray, rapacious old face reminded her queerly of
the old landlady in the Atlantic City boarding-house, the same
landlady-eyes showing the struggle to make allowances for all
humanity and the itch to profit by its failings. Connie found herself arranging the same fixed nervous smile on her face she had
used then, a smile to show she was not afraid at all, she was, oh,
quite at ease, a smile that immediately defeated its purpose and
drew a guarded answer from the other. Connie's head felt dizzy
and light, she tried to keep her mind from going back to her

own runaway but everything in this dim, musty-smelling hallway sent the old sensation of helpless desperation shivering down her spine. She would scarcely have been surprised to see Decker change to Tony before her very eyes, certainly being with him in this place gave her a strangely guilty feeling. She was afraid to meet his embarrassed glance.

"She's up there but the young man is out," said the old woman and added fretfully, "I knew somebody'd be after those kids as soon as I took them in. They showed me their license but I knew there'd be trouble—they had that look. Either somebody'd be after them raising Cain or I'd have to feed 'em myself."

"There won't be any trouble," Decker said with dignity. "I can assure you of that. We only want to talk to them."

He had hoped to stay downstairs while Connie went up, but she clung to his arm so he reluctantly accompanied her to the room at the head of the stairs. Helen's voice, sharp and suspicious, answered their knock. "Who's there! Is it you, Hank?"

She opened it a crack and her face grew set at the sight of her mother.

"So you followed me. . . . Well. . . . Come in."

She wore a new red dress, Connie saw, and she had her hair lacquered to her head in an attempt at sophistication. The bed was unmade with the pasteboard dress box and tissue paper wrapping scattered among the covers.

"At least you have a big easy chair and blue silk curtains," Connie commented, half to herself. "I didn't have anything that nice. . . . And you have a real closet instead of a clothes-tree with cretonne over it."

Yes, Helen's room—so like in spirit the room, in which her mother had once lived—was not so dreary in its actual details. Helen was taken aback by the remark. She relented a little and even beamed at her callers.

"And the curtains slide together by this cord—look!" she demonstrated looking eagerly from one to the other. "And I got this dress and another new one—no, I won't show it to you, you'd say it was too old but I guess I can pick my own clothes now."

She sat down on the edge of the bed and crossed her legs. Connie could only stare at her, not knowing what to say or how to begin.

"You don't need to look at me that way, Mother, and there's no good expecting me to come home 'cause I won't," Helen said belligerently. "Nothing could get me back to that hole. I'm married now and I can do as I like. You can't annul the marriage, either, because if you do Hank promised we'd run away again the very first thing. I don't see what you came for—it won't do you a bit of good."

Connie put out her hands appealingly.

"But, Helen, I wanted to tell you things you didn't realize. What if—"

"There's nothing you need to tell me, Mother—don't be silly."

"You may have to go hungry, you may be wrecking your whole future, Helen—"

"Wrecking my future!" Helen laughed sarcastically. "Staying in that dumb town would have wrecked me if you want to know. How could I ever get near a theater living in the backwoods? How could I ever learn to act there? Never see anything, never hear anything! I suppose you expected me to sit around the rest of my life talking about things that never happened the way you and Miss Murrell and he do! Believe me I'd call my life wrecked if I had to do that—"

Decker was stung into defense.

"My dear girl, you're not on the stage yet, you're just on your honeymoon. What's eloping got to do with this career you speak of? I'm afraid I don't see the connection."

Helen planted her hands on her hips.

"Everything! Can't you see that's the only way I could ever get away from home?" she cried. "I got to make things happen when they don't happen of their own accord. Hank had money saved up to get us on our way—it was really to go to college but Hank doesn't want to go to college, he's sick and tired of school. Pop would never give me a nickel so I had to get married to get out, see? You can't just sit around and wait, you know, and talk about things; I want to be doing them. I hate talk."

"But, Helen—" Connie said feebly. She was already defeated, more than that, she saw that here was no shy, sensitive Constance Greene but someone she could not understand, a cruel and curiously fortunate creature who demanded envy rather than pity.

"Yes, and I've got a job, what's more," Helen flung at them triumphantly. "I went around to the stock company playing here and I got a job right off—leaving for Chicago next week."

"What about Hank?" Connie asked in astonishment. Helen sulked and was silent for a minute. Apparently this consideration had worried her a little.

"Oh, Hank'll be all right. He can go on to Detroit like he wanted to. He thinks it's great for me to go on the stage. He'll understand."

"You haven't told him?" Decker asked, hating her for her assurance, her easy mastery of fate.

"I thought I'd see how he felt first," Helen admitted, twisting her wedding ring. "I thought when he came in I'd hint around and see—after all it's a job and he knows we've got to make money."

"Supposing," pursued Decker, "after you've—ah—hinted at your plan Hank shows he doesn't want you to go? You'd have to give it up then.

"Don't be silly," said Helen impatiently. "I'd just have to go and leave a note, that's all. I wouldn't want to fight with Hank. He'd get used to the idea of my going. Hank's all right."

Connie wanted to laugh, the idea of coming to Helen with help or with warnings was so ridiculous. Helen marrying, not out of foolish infatuation, but by shrewd calculation, knowing each step of the way what to do. And after all—hadn't she run

away with Tony, herself, for the same reason? Yet in Helen she
saw some strange alloy that made her strong where she had
been weak, made her blind to all pain and all pity in the march
toward her goal. She knew almost for a certainty that Helen
would climb the heights she herself had only glimpsed. She
could climb because she had no respect for those heights—only
respect for herself, and she was not to be stopped by considering
where her heel went. For the first time Connie had a sickening
realization of her own failure. She looked around and met
Decker's eye, knew instinctively that he had been struck by the
same thought.

"We were too kind," she murmured to him sadly. "Too
kind to everyone."

"Perhaps to ourselves," Decker answered morosely.

"Well, what about it?" demanded Helen. "Honestly,
Mama, there's no point in trying to get me back home because
I'll never go there. I've got my chance right now and some day
when you see me a leading lady you'll see I was right."

"I think I see it now," said Connie wearily. "I suppose you'll
want us to go so you can tell Hank about your job—alone."

Helen was softened by her mother's surrender.

"I have to see the manager first. And you might take me to
lunch. I told Hank I'd just have a sandwich but if you're going
to a restaurant. . . ."

She pulled on a little velvet hat—new, too, Connie saw—
and hurried them out.

"There's a rotisserie down the street. We went there last
night."

Decker held Connie's arm for she was trembling visibly as
they walked down the street. They were quiet while Helen,
now assured of peace so far as her family was concerned, chattered of her interview with the Stock Company manager, how
he complimented her on her looks, what a fine way she carried
herself, how well she could wear clothes, what a fine dramatic
quality he detected in her voice. . . .

In the window of the rotisserie an enormous chef stood, and Connie watched him fastening the chickens to the spit with his great hands. As they ate she dimly heard Helen's boasting and her great plans against a background of this revolving spit and the smell of frying chicken fat. She felt sick and unhappy as if someone had shaken her by the shoulders and shouted, "See, you weren't good enough! Say what you will about Fate and all that, you just weren't good enough. Too soft."

She saw Decker through a blur of tears and without touching him knew that they were closer than they had ever been, that he, too, was glad at least they were together. . . . He wanted to tell her about the rotisserie Ilsa Darmster had discovered. He wanted to talk about the difference between French and Italian cooking, what wines were best served with fowl, but Helen's chilling presence intervened, her hard, cool voice came between them like the cold nose of a revolver, ominous, real. . . . He wanted them to be back again in Dell River so that they could really enjoy this strange expedition and he hated Helen for her savage self-sufficiency.

As they went out Connie lingered behind to watch the chef impale a new batch of broilers. His hands fascinated her, their routine movements soothed her nerves. She saw that he was looking at her with a half-smile and she gripped the counter-rail in sudden recognition.

"Tony!"

"Sure," he nodded toward Decker and Helen now at the door. "Better go ahead—your friends have gone."

"Did you see the notices I put in the paper? I wanted to see you."

"Sure, I saw 'em." He salted a pail of French-fried potatoes. He had grown enormously fat, Connie afterward could not understand how she came to recognize him except for the great brown eyes and perhaps the special delicacy of his great hands.

"You didn't answer."

He shrugged.

"I been too busy. . . Too busy then . . . too busy now. . .
Look—your friends—"

Connie hesitated.

"I'm glad you're happy . . . glad I saw you again. Do you—
do you miss the carnival life?"

He frowned at her and leaned forward confidentially.

"Say, that was no life. . . .This is the business. Wish'd I'd
started in it earlier. . . .My wife helps, too. . . . She's in the back. . . ."

There was nothing more to say. Whatever she had ever
wanted to know was answered now. "Well—goodbye—Tony."

He was relieved.

"So long, signora."

He had forgotten her name, Connie reflected, hurrying
after Decker and Helen. Helen announced that she was going
to go to the building next door to see her manager again and
was ready to say goodbye immediately.

"What were you saying to that awful man, Mama?" she
wanted to know.

"I only asked how the machine worked," Connie murmured.

Helen burst into a peal of laughter.

"Mama, you are such a ninny!" she exclaimed almost affectionately. "Here's where I go. Goodbye . . . Oh, say, you can give
my green pocketbook to Mimi—all my new clothes are red."

She darted into a doorway. Connie and Decker walked
slowly back to the depot, both of them tired out, as if they had
been on a long, long journey.

☙

On The Oaks' front porch Miss Swasey and Miss Emmons
whispered their conjectures about Professor Decker, while
Louisa pretended to read. He ran in and out of the place like a
man possessed, speaking to no one, half the time not even rec-
ognizing friends who addressed him. It was all very well to

diagnose all this as "genius" but his nervous condition was far too obviously related to Mrs. Benjamin's illness. She had collapsed after her expedition to Greentown, the doctor from Greentown was there every day and Mimi was kept out of school to take charge of the house. There were even days—the whole town knew this—when the sick woman was allowed to see no one and on such days the music teacher might be seen rushing through the streets swinging his cane, his necktie flying, his hat askew, his face so desperately pale that no one had the heart to take him to task for his eccentric behavior. He waited in the cobbler shop hours for Gus to come downstairs and report on her condition; his hands unconsciously went through the "Campanella" on the work-table. Rehearsals for the Commencement music were forgotten and students waited in vain for their special lessons.

He would not talk to Louisa about this dark disaster in the air for even Louisa was morbidly pessimistic about the outcome. He, Decker, was certain that Connie Benjamin could not die but the thought held such frightening possibilities that he could not sleep. In one way he resented the illness—a charming game carried beyond the bounds of good taste; after all one may vary friendship with separations, quarrels, and sickness but at no point is it permissible to prolong worry to such an agonizing pitch. At night he could not endure the intimate living room of The Oaks with the Misses Swasey and Emmons so anxious to discuss the Benjamin family with him. He would scarcely touch his supper and would leave abruptly to call at the cobbler shop upstairs, if possible, then to roam in the darkness along the river bank, swishing at the bushes with his cane, stumbling blindly over stumps and broken fences. Night after night Louisa threw on a dark cape and slipped out of the house to follow him, alarmed by his haggard appearance. She would stop at the church gate, seeing him go on into the fields, then strain her eyes to follow him in the moonlight. She knew he always lingered by the old Benjamin house now occupied by a young married couple given to noisy card parties and much entertainment When he was back in sight again she could breathe easily and slip quietly back to The Oaks again.

"What was there between them to make him so upset by her being sick?" Miss Emmons pondered aloud more than once.

"Nothing," Louisa was almost despairing of making people believe. "They were only friends—it was because they both loved music."

"But don't I love music too?" Miss Emmons loudly argued. "Didn't I take lessons all my life and don't I go to concerts in Cincinnati every time I visit my cousin? And haven't I told him so a dozen times? That doesn't make him friendly with me does it? No, sir, there's something more."

She caught Miss Swasey's eye and Miss Swasey nodded complete agreement.

"Then I don't know," Louisa surrendered but her heart was heavy. Now they no longer teased her about the music teacher and first she was relieved, then a dreadful empty sensation followed. If she had not the town's belief that Decker was rather specially hers, then she had nothing, certainly she had no private assurances to sustain her. All she had had was the reputation for being in love with him; now that reputation was vanishing and she felt as deprived as if it had been a real love. She could hear him muttering to himself at night in the room adjoining and sometimes she got up and crouched beside the wall whispering, "You poor darling—there—there!"

One night she was out in the hall when he unexpectedly opened the door and saw her there.

"I heard you walking about," Louisa apologized in a whisper. "I thought you might need a bromide."

Decker blinked at her as if trying to remember just where this little woman in a brown wrapper, her braids down her back, could possibly belong. He brushed a hand over his forehead.

"I don't want to sleep, thanks," he said. "There are too many things for me to think about."

Louisa sought to distract him.

"Arrangements for your summer?" He seized upon the idea gratefully.

"Exactly," he said. "I'm making some important decisions."

She waited till he closed the door before creeping back to her room. She could not think of Mrs. Benjamin except through him—even while she tried to imagine Connie's pain she knew she was thinking for Decker, loaning him her heart and her own pity as if his were not enough for this major assignment. Here, take my strength to put with yours, take my heart to relieve yours. . . .

"Poor, poor darling," thought Louisa, because his swagger had vanished and he was such a shrinking, forlorn little man. She loved him for being so plainly not a romantic figure, not a hero.

꙳

Footsteps going up and down the stairs, up and down, creaking tiptoe, cautiously hurrying, sounded in Connie's head as if they were connected with the painful beating of her heart. She could lull the pain by staring fixedly at the rainbow window until the colors raced after each other in a dizzy blur, but a look in this direction meant a contact with Mimi's white little face, and this required a reassuring smile almost beyond her strength. So Connie kept her eyes fixed on the wall before her where a diamond-shaped mirror hung and so she waited for the peaceful split second between the agonizing heartbeats. The mirror swung to and fro like a pendulum and shrunk from the size of a house to the size of a tiny jewel, yes, a diamond, whose corners were intolerably sharp, a diamond that was lost in her chest somewhere, its tiny points stabbing her with each breath. This was not true, of course, it was only that she was so in the habit of transforming what she saw into amusing images for Decker. When he came in the room she knew she had only to point to the mirror and he would know what she meant, he would perhaps put it into the very same words she would have used. Another thing about the mirror was the way it presented faces to her before the owners of these faces came into the room. There was a door in this mirror, for instance, a door that was somehow familiar but it was too tiresome to connect it with a real door so it was just a magic one. Sometimes it opened just a few inches and a terrified face would look silently down at her—Mrs. Busch, Laurie Neville, Louisa, Gus, Doctor Arnold. The face would remain just a moment or two with alarm and pity shining in its eyes, then it vanished and the real face would appear, smiling, complete with owner, at the head of the bedside. Connie thought, "When I get better I must remember to laugh at this. It's such a joke my spying on people before they put their faces on. . . ."

She must tell Decker. She was glad she had so much to tell him now. There were her impressions of physical pain. There really was such a thing, it appeared, and when you had it you could not help knowing that that was what you were meant for—a body was marked like a baking measure for how much pain it could hold and then it was efficiently filled to the brim. Decker, Decker, where are you? . . .

He was there and she could smile at him but breath was too priceless to risk speaking. She was getting used to the pain—at first it had been accompanied by surprise; it was undignified, people should not have diamonds in their chests for hearts to stumble upon in their frantic beating. . . . With Decker beside her and his expression revealing that he forgave her this unfortunate error and was as sure as she was that we do not die—parents, friends, yes, but *we* do not die, though it would make a fine discussion sometime (she must remember every little detail of the fear to describe to him). She had so many things to tell him—she couldn't think of them now, but new things kept popping up in her mind—the way her grandfather's hand shook lifting a teacup, the clear-cut profile of a nun—Sister Bertha!—fancy that name flying through space to her. It had

been years since she'd thought of Sister Bertha . . . her very
voice came to her . . . her first singing lesson. . . . Connie looked
at Decker eagerly but she could not spare the breath to tell him
about Sister Bertha or the diamond, she must use it for something more important, something she'd just thought about
Gus—yes, she could almost laugh at it now and Decker surely
would—that Gus had never believed in her, he only knew he'd
picked her up, a girl in trouble, in Atlantic City, and he was
willing to overlook her past since she made him a good wife . . .
that was really funny, wasn't it? . . . Tony would have been like
that too. . . . She should have told Decker about Tony in the
cafeteria. That was funny . . . Oh, it was amazing how much
she had to tell him. In a minute she would speak—she'd save
enough breath to tell him.

When Dr. Arnold's face flashed on the mirror she thought,
"This must be the way one dies. People collect on a mirror like
dust and something rushes through your mind emptying all the
drawers and shelves to see if you're leaving anything behind—a
Sister Bertha or a Mrs. Busch." . . . Do you remember, Decker,
the day Busch said, "That was the loveliest music I ever
heard?" . . . That was the day I sang—"See the waves of fair
Sorrento—What a treasure lies beneath them—" Manuel's
song. . . .

Now Dr. Arnold was sitting on the side of the bed but she
could see Decker behind him. There were other people near but
there was so little time for anyone but Decker, so many things to
tell him. When she caught his eye she knew he understood, he
forgave her for not telling him all at once, he understood about
the mirror, about the diamond, about Sister Bertha. . . . In Dr.
Arnold's black eyes she saw herself tiny, tiny enough to fit into
the mirror at its very smallest, dwindled away to nothing. So
this was the end. What a pity, she thought, no one will ever
know these are my last thoughts—that Dr. Arnold's mouth was
so small. . . . *And* so little (very different from small) and his
necktie was so blue, so amazingly blue. You couldn't breathe for

the pain of looking at such blue. Please, oh please, please not so blue. . . . And a bell tingling somewhere was a sensation further off than the sharp agony in her chest, the soft splintering of rhythmic bombs in her heart, splintering into stars of almost perfect pain. . . . Her body was not big enough to hold such feeling. How do birds die, Decker, when they have such little hearts?—not big enough really for more than a few beats and certainly no space left for pain. . . . The doctor's little mouth—his teeny, tiny mouth—how perfectly ridiculous! She would like to tell Decker these last thoughts, these sudden revelations. My dear, she would say, you've no idea how perfectly ridiculous. . . . But that was not what she wanted to say to Decker. . . . She must not waste words, especially when there was that one very important message for him. She'd forgotten what it was but it buzzed about in her head—she almost captured it once when she met Decker's eye and then the doctor came between and it was lost. . . . She detached herself from her body, it was so riddled with bombs one might as well leave it, but already she ached with missing it. The pain of separation was exactly like the real pain in her heart—perhaps that was what she meant to tell him, but that was wrong, she knew it when she saw his blue eyes again and felt him groping desperately for her hand as if at last he must find something tangible about her to hold. . . . She felt the words forming in her mouth—she could not be sure they were her words or his words, but they were exactly what she wanted to say, that most important thing—

"Dear—my dear—"

That must have been right for he bent over and kissed her hand—Deckers do not do that except for the right words. . . . Now his blue eyes again. Blue that broke your heart, that made your ragged breath catch once more, that stabbing blue that would not relent but swam nearer and nearer until there was no escape. Connie saw her thin white fingers flung out frantically against it, a thin little white fan caught in the blue, fading into it and then quite lost in it—quite lost.

✧

He was on the steamer. He was not the village music teacher, he was Blaine Decker, cosmopolite, that young man who showed such promise at the Conservatory and who later—as the intimate friend of Starr Donnell, the writer, played charmingly in one or two important drawing-rooms in Paris. Once he had not been able to enjoy a situation until he had put it into its best form in his mind, but now—with no fascinated listener in mind he could see no advantage in his position, he was just a dazed man going through the motions of a long-familiar dream—a dream that had been so dear that the reality was hopelessly dull in comparison. He was not happy in the fulfilment—he was lonely for the dream. He missed the little apartment over the cobbler shop where he could wish so much finer wishes than this. He could not feel properly grateful to Laurie Neville for arranging the trip; it was clever and kind of her to make the gift so simply as if it were a loan—he had been too crushed by the last few weeks to refuse, but he was not grateful. Here he was on his way to two years in Europe and all he could feel was a hideous sense of loss and resentment that his private life had been invaded—he was being forced to make good a promissory note. Vaguely he knew that his own far country—which Laurie Neville could know nothing about— was tangled irretrievably with Connie Benjamin's; it was not Paris or Munich or Milan—those were only the working names for this charming place. It was not fair to be asked to check up on it. Connie would have understood.

He wandered around the deck, his muffler flying in the breeze, his new topcoat flapping about his knees, his tie—as always—flying gaily from side to side. In six more days he would be in Paris—oh terrifying thought! It was no longer a city of dreams set in the silvery mist of romantic memories but a strange unfriendly place that had once found him not good enough; it was only back in Dell River that Paris belonged to

him completely, a tender place that loved him, that perpetually
held out arms to him. . . . And Starr. . . . He had discovered that
Starr was living in Paris again. In the steamer dining room an
Englishwoman he did not remember came up to his table and
reminded him that they had met abroad years ago. She'd seen
Starr last winter in Italy.

"You'll be staying with him?" she inquired.

"It's possible," murmured Decker, feeling pushed by this
woman into something he was not at all sure he wanted just as
Laurie had pushed him. Did he want to see Starr? . . . Of course
he would call at the old address. He would stand in the downstairs hallway waiting for the "Who is it?—Come on up!" with
that same old feeling of not being equal to Starr's friends . . . he
would take a deep breath on each landing to brace himself for
the plunge—keep guard on himself so that no naive spontane-
ity should escape. . . . How could he look up Starr when he had
forgotten the Waldstein Sonata, his fingers stumbled over the
Military Polonaise, how could he explain he'd been teaching the
Pilgrims' Chorus?

"So you're back," Starr would say with his queer restrained
smile—decently bred people never betrayed childish joy. "Well,
well! Here you are, everybody, here's old Blaine Decker back
from the American jungle. He'll play for us presently. . . ."

No, he wasn't prepared for Starr, he wasn't prepared for
Europe or leisure, either. He was being rushed into all sorts of
things with no chance to savor them. Laurie had hurried him
into this trip, the woman yonder was pushing him back to
Starr—Starr would force him back into his old professional
ambition for you must do—do—do—to justify Starr's friendship. Starr was bored by amiable nobodies. He drove you to
agonizing ambition.

Aimlessly Decker drifted down to his cabin and closed the
door. On the washstand lay the books from Miss Manning. He
picked them up and examined the titles. Novels. He'd never
liked novels but probably Starr's crowd would talk about them

so he'd better read them. . . . On the bed was the package from Louisa Murrell. A volume of Swinburne. He sat down and turned it over in his hand, fighting back a wave of unutterable loneliness, a nostalgia for Connie Benjamin's soothing flattery and the sweet drug of their mutual consolations. Now that he was on his way to Paris he could think only of Dell River, the lazy little Park, the twisted tree behind the cobbler shop, the Benjamins' ragged garden, the haunting fragrance of locust blossoms . . . No, Connie Benjamin was not gone. Nothing could ever happen to him that he would not know exactly what she would have said about it. He would never be alone again for he would have her in his brain, in his very veins—to every song he ever heard there would be two people listening.

The foghorn blew harshly and Decker looked about the little room, puzzled for a moment. Ah yes, Paris. . . . But Paris wasn't the real place. That was now Dell River—the place he had just left.

Also by Dawn Powell

ANGELS ON TOAST

THE GOLDEN SPUR

THE LOCUSTS HAVE NO KING

MY HOME IS FAR AWAY

A TIME TO BE BORN

THE WICKED PAVILION

ᔓ

DAWN POWELL AT HER BEST
Including the novels DANCE NIGHT
and TURN, MAGIC WHEEL and selected stories

THE DIARIES OF DAWN POWELL: 1931-1965

A NOTE ON THE BOOK

The text for this book was composed by
Steerforth Press using a digital version of
Granjon, a typeface designed by George W.
Jones and first issued by Linotype in 1928. The
book was printed on acid free papers and
bound by Quebecor Printing~Book Press Inc.
of North Brattleboro, Vermont.